1

THE TIDEWAITER

By
Robert Cottrell

Printed by Aziumuth Printers of Bristol
Published May 2018

"I would like to congratulate you on having completed a literary endeavour of this magnitude. It is not at all easy to write, and to write a novel that is so entertaining while being so informative is a monumental task indeed."

Pure Knowledge Solution LLP

Price £9.50

I dedicate this book to Peter Stone,
In addition, Michael Laws (a Thames waterman)

Peter Stone will not believe how much sleep
I lost in trying to formulate the plot.

Sir Richard Sharpe appears by permission
of Bernard Cornwell, although the author
doubted if his character would
ever have accepted the honour of a knighthood.

I wish to thank Paper True for their excellent
work in editing this novel. Without them the book
would probably have rapidly descended into utter rubbish.

Also good friends from Shropshire, who know who they are.

George Maynard wearing the coveted regalia of Thomas Doggett.

CHAPTER 1

13 th October 1825

The weather this year had been extremely changeable. In February, we had major storms, followed by a very hot summer. The storms came back vigorously in August, and today, the thirteenth day of October 1825, the weather was so cold that snow was predicted to fall within days. In fact, snow did fall a week after my apprenticeship binding to George Wyld, an Uncle by marriage to Aunt Martha. My father could have become my master, but he thought it best for me to be bound to Uncle George. I found this hard to understand, but I believed this was because he had already lost a son to drowning. I later ascertained that if father had had way, he would have wanted me to take up a trade unrelated to the river.

The family had only just got over the death, last year, of my Uncle John, caused by an accident when his boat came downstream under London Bridge. An incoming barge clipped the quarter of his wherry, and sunk his craft. His body was recovered within a few days off Rotherhithe. Thankfully, our family was able to hold a dignified funeral for him at St.Mary's Church, Lambeth. The coroner's court recorded a verdict of death by misadventure, but I know the family had reservations.

Uncle John had been a Customhouse waterman, or as our family called it, 'a tidewaiter'. His wife, Elizabeth, always considered the term hilarious, as her husband was always away working. Being seldom at home, he was unable to do any household chores.

I walked with my parents, Charles Henry and Charlotte Maynard, from the family home at Lambeth to Saint Mary at Hill and Watermen's Hall, crossing over to the north shore at London Bridge. The river was extremely busy - every conceivable type of vessel covered the surface of the Thames - the majority being fully laden hay barges making their way inwards from the farmlands of Essex and East Anglia. Empty barges were sailing downstream to load cargoes, hay being the main commodity. It looked like we were in for a hard winter.

When we had almost reached Watermen's Hall, mother took out her handkerchief, spat on it, and tried to clean my face and re-arrange my hair before entering the building. The things mothers do to embarrass their children! Not that I was a child - I was a couple of weeks past my fourteenth birthday. My two younger brothers, Robert and William, accompanied us, while my eldest living brother, Henry, waited for us within the Hall's main entrance. He had been apprenticed to father two years earlier. When it was my turn to be apprenticed, father decided the trade was too dangerous. If I wanted to work as lighterman or waterman, I had to find my own master. My brother Henry was due to return to the Hall in a few months. He had to be verbally examined regarding his river knowledge prior to obtaining his provisional two-year licence.

As far as I knew, the Maynard family had worked on the river. My eldest brother Charles Henry would have been twenty-four years of age now. He had been apprenticed to father ten years earlier. Sadly, my brother drowned during a violent storm whilst rowing through Westminster Bridge.

Our family had more than its fair share of accidents. Mother outwardly accepted the risks of the trade, but I knew she kept her fears to herself.

My father was bound in 1777 to his father, and my grandfather had been apprenticed in 1745. As I have said, our family went way back.

George Wyld was waiting just inside the stone passageway leading to the small parlour room where today's bindings would occur. The Court Beadle had a quick word with Uncle George and father, who ushered me in front of the Clerk of the Court. I walked into the parlour room, with Uncle George and stood to attention in front of the Master of the Watermen's Company with his two Wardens either side.

The clerk opened the page of the apprenticeship-binding book and wrote the following:-

"George Wyld, of Lambeth, bound his apprentice George Maynard for 7 years beginning 13th October 1825."

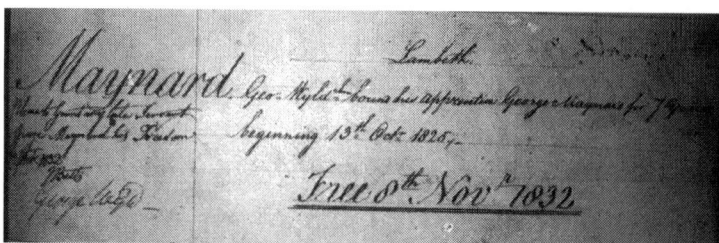

A copy of George Maynard's binding.

That was that.

I was now bound to George Wyld for the next seven years. There must have been close to forty-five lads bound that day. Like my brother Henry, I would have to return after two years to be verbally tested on my river knowledge, and with some luck obtain my provisional license. At the end of my seven-year term, I would return to the Hall for another examination, whereby I hoped to receive my freedom. There were stringent rules that every apprentice had to agree to – "no gambling, no drinking, no play houses and no fornication" and so on - but at least my new master had to agree not to feed me salmon more than three times a week. Can you imagine eating that cheap revolting fish more than once a week, let alone three!

Normally an apprentice was clothed and cared for within his master's household, but as George was my uncle, he was happy for me to remain at my parent's house. I wondered how many times I would be eating salmon at home.

As it was nearing mid-day, I hoped Uncle George would tell me my training would commence first light in the morning - but no! He ordered me to beach his boats that very afternoon on a sandy shore, not mud, to give them a thorough scrub, both inside and out, with a stiff broom.

The first step of my training would be to learn all the reaches downstream from Teddington to Gravesend. In former times, all apprentices had to know the reaches and points as far upstream as Windsor. In addition to this, I had to be aware of the increasing number of bridges that traversed the Thames, their working arches, and how the wind and tide might affect the tidal flow when travelling up and downstream for each bridge. Above all, I had to remember every buoy, their colours shapes and meanings along with every plying place. Coming from a large river family, I knew most of them already, with the exception of those below Greenwich. I had rarely been downstream the lower side of Greenwich, unlike Uncle John. As a tidewaiter, he had been principally assigned at Gravesend, where he patiently waited for continental ships entering the Thames. Uncle John had to inspect the cargoes to ascertain the correct taxation.

Within a few months, my master suggested that as I was approaching fifteen, I should journey downstream to Gravesend to be accustomed with the numerous plying places the lower side of Greenwich. He recommended leaving Lambeth on the top of the tide, thereby taking full advantage of the ebb tide all the way downstream to Gravesend. I did not over like his proposal of sleeping overnight in the *Lady Martha* to catch the first of the flood tide the following morning to return to Lambeth. It made me happier when he suggested that another apprentice, James Kippen should accompany me. James, like me, came from Lambeth. Better still, we had been apprenticed on the same day.

Uncle George had four or five wherries; the oldest and smallest boat was called the *Lady Martha* named after his wife. It was about twenty foot long, with a beam of eight. It was a teak clinker-built boat with a reasonable freeboard, making rowing safer in the heavier swells of Gravesend.

We had to wait until the end of May before making our first excursion to Gravesend, for the most part due to the river freezing at Deptford earlier that year. After checking the paraffin navigation lamps and wicks, and making sure, we had sufficient mooring ropes, bailers, a boathook and rope fenders, we departed from Paris Garden stairs at Lambeth just after sunrise on the twenty-eighth day of May. James and I took turns at rowing until we reached Greenwich. We scribbled notes as we passed the numerous plying places, all of which were well known to both of us. However, we were about to journey into the unknown - we passed Blackwall, Charlton, Woolwich, and Erith.

At Erith causeway, we rested and ate. In comparison with what we had already passed, there seemed to be less stairs and causeways downstream from Woolwich. We hoped this would make our training considerably easier. There were fewer causeways at Greenhithe, Swanscombe and Northfleet, and before long, the church of Saint George at Gravesend came into view.

I hated Gravesend. It seemed strange compared to Lambeth. The air was much sweeter than in London, and the people appeared friendly enough, but it was very different from Lambeth. When we finally arrived at Gravesend, we moored alongside an empty collar barge moored offshore from the Three Daws. There was a plying place on the upper side of the riverside tavern. However, Uncle George advised us not to go ashore. He deemed it

16

far too dangerous due to the activities of the press gang. Like mother's bedtime stories, he enjoyed telling us that the navy's press gang loved to gobble up watermen and lightermen, especially a stupid apprentice or two. Suffice it to say - we remained aboard the *Lady Martha* all night under dry sailcloth.

Next morning, after a meagre breakfast, we let go our mooring ropes and proceeded back home, with the assistance of the strong flood tide. On our return journey, we made notes of the north shore stairs and causeways. The mud flats extending nigh on midstream made it impossible to construct riverside stairs until we reached Thurrock and Purfleet. Virtually every causeway on the lower side of Woolwich had been in a poor state of repair - covered in mud and green-brown slime.

On our long journey home, we passed the usual multitude of dead animals bobbing on the surface of the river, but thankfully, it was nowhere as bad as Lambeth. Lambeth may have smelt like death, but at least it was home.

Another day was chosen during the following month when the tides would be right for our journey, and the trip was duplicated. We concentrated our efforts on the south shore stairs on our outward row and the north shore when returning home. In common with river tradition, Jimmy did not mind me calling him "Kipper" as a jolly nickname; in turn, his nickname for me was "Mayday".

On our fourth voyage, we decided it was time to be brave and go ashore. We securely moored the *'Lady Martha'*, fore and aft, alongside the stairs off the Town Pier near the Three Daws, and took our first tentative steps on Gravesend soil, - straight into alarming shouts of, "Where the bloody hell are you two buggers going?"

CHAPTER 2

The Three Daws

An early photograph of the Three Daws at Gravesend

We stood perfectly still, each of us held by a vice-like grip on the shoulder. We turned our heads to find soldiers from the local garrison glaring at us. Solomon Ribbens, the owner of the Three Daws had armed himself with a heavy cudgel standing menacing at their sides, his wife Margaret looking equally threatening with her frying-pan one-step behind them, it was easy to see who the master of the house was.

So much for Gravesend hospitality!

Kipper heard it first - a noise - no, a quiet cough. Not a sickly wheezing cough, it was more of "I am here cough." Behind Margaret Ribbens, an authoritative voice gave an order. "At ease privates, you seem to be scaring our guests."

The soldiers immediately released their grips and stood at ease.

"Grant, Burn, thank you men, you may return to your duties at the blockhouse," the voice continued.

Private Grant was about to protest, but the unknown voice continued speaking "You are both improperly dressed with unbuttoned tunics, and why should there be a strong smell of alcohol on your breath." Both men returned to the blockhouse without further objections. Solomon Ribbens gave a stupid salute while his left hand quickly attempted to hide his heavy weapon beneath his beer-stained apron.

Kipper whispered to me that he was not scared, but the stranger had already noticed a pool of yellowish liquid by Kipper's boots. However, the new comer decided not to embarrass Kipper and averted his head towards Solomon and Margaret Ribbens, glaring at the latter retreating as she dashed back to her kitchen.

The stranger came into full view as he slowly circled the two young apprentices. He was immaculately dressed in civilian clothes, but he had the airs of a high-ranking soldier. Solomon immediately recognised the man and called him "Your Lordship," giving him a clumsy court bow, much to the annoyance of the as yet to be introduced man. Ribbens began to whistle a nondescript tune to hide his nervousness. "Boys, this is his Lordship Sir Richard Sharpe," Ribbens hurriedly spurted out.

Sir Richard Sharpe stood directly in front of the two lads enquiring if either of them could read or write. The question became clear when Sir Richard pointed at a signpost and said, "Did you not see the sign on the mooring stairs - no unauthorised moorings?" The interrogation, if that is what it was, continued gently with Sir Richard requesting our names. Turning brash out of fear, Kipper answered first, stating his name was James Kippen, waterman apprentice of Lambeth. I quickly followed by saying "George Maynard sir, waterman apprentice also from Lambeth." The addition of the word "Sir" appeared to ease the unexpected confrontation. My father had always told me that manners went a long way and didn't cost anything.

Solomon enquired what Sir Richard wanted to do about the altercation and if he should call for the local constabulary. Sir Richard, who enquired if either of us could count simply ignored Solomon's question. The question appeared bizarre, but we answered simultaneously with a firm "Yes sir."

"Good, then I will enjoy fresh conversation. Will you both join me for supper? However, as both of you are apprentices, I think it best if we retire to the riverside restaurant. Don't want either of you to be in trouble with the law or your masters do we" Sir Richard waved away our protests about not having any coins with us, telling us we were his guests.

Solomon Ribbens guided us to an empty table, by the window, within the riverside terrace and suggested some fine ham and cheeses that he had had delivered that very afternoon. Solomon respectfully suggested the salmon for the lads but Sir Richard politely notified Ribbens that we would all eat the ham and cheese.

"Bring a jug of ale and some watered down ale or if they prefer fresh spring water for the boys" he ordered.

Noticing that we were curious about who our esteemed benefactor was, Solomon Ribbens formerly introduced us to His Lordship, Sir Richard Sharpe a veterinary of the Peninsular Wars and Waterloo. We both giggled at Ribbens mispronunciation. "Tarnation Ribbens, you know full well I am not a Lord, plain Sir will do!" After Ribbens had left for the kitchen to assist his wife, Sir Richard turned to us, exclaiming, "Dratted bootlicker - he will be the death of me." Margaret Ribbens returned with three plates of thickly carved ham and various cheeses, fresh baked bread and churned butter, together with three knives and forks. Solomon carried a jug of ale and two glasses of home-made lemonade. Solomon quickly departed, still whistling to himself. The proprietor was evidently still nervous in front of Sir Richard.

Kipper asked Sir Richard if he had caught sight of the monster at Waterloo, to which he replied, "Sorry lads didn't see any monster, just one clever Emperor trying to outwit us. His tactics were sound; his undoing was the atrocious weather and his splitting his forces. If the battle had commenced an hour earlier he would have been victorious, and we would all have been buried beneath the mud in a far-off foreign field. It was a damn close thing though, but luck was on our side within a Belgian field just south of the town of Waterloo."

Solomon returned, to check if more drinks were needed, on the house of course. This was a blatant lie, as Sir Richard had noticed a group of watermen talking to Ribbens, telling him to serve us with a round of drinks on them. Naturally, Sir Richard assumed the drinks were for his benefit, but he was wrong. It was for mine. One of the watermen strolled over to our table and introduced himself to me - his name was William Martin and had heard the commotion outside and been told my name was Maynard, related to the John Maynard who had recently drowned under London Bridge. Martin was a waterman and owned a bumboat the *'Henrietta,'* named after his wife. The bumboatman wished to convey his condolences and told me that my Uncle, despite being a tidewaiter, or customs man, was a good and decent man.

Our conversation was yet again disturbed by a commotion outside the Daws. Looking out, we saw a group of armed sailors trying to snare two local lads, not much older than us. Sir Richard banged on the window gesturing the gang to piss-off. "Bloody press gang," he cursed, "at least the army offers the King's shilling."

We sat the best part of the early evening chatting with Sir Richard Sharpe. Not that he was a friend, but he was surprisingly good company and did not mind chatting with us common lads. Just before he was about to depart, I asked him why he had enquired if we could count. He purposely waited until Solomon Ribbens returned before replying. "I have taken supper at the Daws every Thursday for the past five weeks, and when it is time to settle my account, despite ordering the same food and drink every week the total has never been the same. I am sure Solomon makes the prices up as he goes along, or maybe he finds counting too taxing."

I liked Richard Sharpe; he was a good man who didn't make us feel out of our depth. I enquired of him what it was like to be knighted and be a "Sir". His answer was totally unexpected and witty – "Just because the King of England tickles your shoulder with a sword and makes you a Knight of the Realm, you don't become any different. We are still all the same - flesh and blood, no better and no worse than the next man."

Sir Richard bid us farewell and returned to his lodgings by the blockhouse, as the two of us returned to the comforts of the 'Lady Martha' in the hope of a good night's sleep.

Just after sunrise the following morning, the tide began to flood, and our journey back home to Lambeth would begin. However, during the night, another vessel had moored alongside the 'Lady Martha' making it impossible for us to leave. The skipper of the other vessel, the 'Henrietta', made his presence known and kindly offered both of us a mug of hot strong tea before setting off. At the same time Bill Martin, who we had met the previous evening in the Daws, gave me a newspaper cutting from a copy of the Penny Post reporting on the death of John Maynard. It read.

"On Tuesday morning, as John Maynard, a custom-house waterman, passed under London Bridge, a barge, which was passing through the centre arch at the same time, run over the wherry in which Maynard was, and upset her. Before any assistance could be rendered to the unfortunate man, he fell a victim to a watery grave."

I neatly folded the newspaper cutting and returned it to Bill Martin, who put it into his coat pocket. Bill patted me gently on the shoulder. At the same time, he gave me a brief smile and apologised if his action had upset me in any way, assuring me that had not been his intention. Sipping hot tea in the stern of the *'Lady Martha'* was a pleasant distraction from remembering the loss of my uncle in such tragic circumstances as the newspaper portrayed.

Kipper finished his tea and got up to sort out the mooring lines ready for our departure. Bill Martin came aft to sit with me for a brief talk. Once again, he told me how honest and helpful my uncle had been. He always had time to talk to anyone who needed a word of advice. The conversation appeared to have no point other than to tell me I should have been proud of Uncle John.

I shouted to Kipper to make ready to let all our headlines and forward spring rope go while I let go our last rope, the back spring. Bill was about step over the gunwale of the *'Lady Martha'* to board his own vessel, when he suddenly turned and said with much concern, "I think your uncle worried about something the last time I saw him. He was certainly concerned for his own safety. Whether this had anything to do with his accident I cannot comment, but it was not the John Maynard that I knew who left Gravesend. We did not see him again after that; just read about his death in the papers.

25

If you wish, young Maynard, I can make enquires down here, unless you don't want to drag up old memories."

With that, Bill Martin boarded the *'Henrietta'* and waved to us as we departed Gravesend. In return I gave a half hearted waive and Kipper, feeling warmed from his hot mug of tea, gave a jolly cheerful wave, and started to act the fool, he held his battered tin mug aloof as if it were a trophy and showed it off in the middle of the *'Lady Martha'*. When Kipper realised his actions were out of order, he quickly calmed down and sat beside me, ready to take up his oar. He glanced at me and noticed tears running down my cheeks, but being a good friend he said nothing except – "Let's go home Mayday."

Lambeth might smell, but it was home.

CHAPTER 3

October 1827

I thought my training had gone well, especially above London Bridge, which included knowledge on the working spans for inward and outgoing vessels. However, my weak point was my grasp of the riverside stairs, especially in Woolwich Reach, which was to my mind problematical. My uncle considered me ready to take my two-year examination, but I expressed concern about the sheer number of plying places the lower side of Blackwall Point. In terms of weather, 1827 had been a good year, so my uncle agreed that a journey downstream to Erith and back would be beneficial to both Kipper and me.

We chose a day to row downstream to Blackwall Point and beyond. We drifted with the tide to enable both of us to test our knowledge. An old causeway immediately the lower side of the Greenwich peninsular seemed to be in a poor state of repair. Next came numerous causeways at Charlton and the Anchor and Hope Hotel, Hardens Manorway came next, followed by two stairs at Trinity, the Dockyard stairs, Nile Street stairs, Hog Lane, Bell Watergate, Warren Lane and Ship and Half Moon stairs and causeways followed in quick succession. Thankfully, there were fewer stairs on the north shore, but we still had to be aware of their locations. We navigated towards the north shore after we cleared the notorious prison hulks.

On the foredeck of the prison hulk, *Dromedary,* Kipper noticed an officer shouting and frantically waving his arms in the air, like a windmill in a gale. We couldn't decide if he wanted us to keep clear or come closer, we concluded that his arms indicated the latter. Once we pulled alongside the old hulk, the stench of human waste became intolerable. However, of course, the poor souls on board were not there to enjoy themselves - most of the prisoners were awaiting transportation to Australia and our other colonies.

Lieutenant Weaver, an excitable young officer, not that much older than Kipper or me, formaly introduced himself and demanded we take a cargo ashore in the '*Lady Martha'* to the military base at the Woolwich Arsenal. Before we could answer, a boarding net unfurled over the gunwale of the prison hulk, and two marines scrambled down its side and into our boat. This was quickly followed by a large bundle lowered down to us wrapped up in bloodied sailcloth. The marine guards both greeted us with a big smile and explained that they had been waiting over an hour for a boat to take the dead body ashore. Lieutenant Weaver gave a wave and threw a small bag into the boat which contained some rations and two silver shillings.

We rowed as fast as we could to the Arsenal, where the guards carried the dead body ashore but not before assuring us that, the deceased had not gone to his maker with the plague. "If you cheat at cards, you expect to get a good bashing or a broken neck."

We quickly departed the Arsenal jetty and navigated across the river to the Old Bargehouse causeway. Salvation Buoy causeway and stairs came next followed by the two stairs at North Woolwich. We then continued upstream to the causeway at West Ham, and finally Hook Ness.

It was at West Ham stairs that three vessels departed for the New World in December 1606 with one hundred and five brave souls aboard. The three vessels were exceptionally small, the largest of which was the one hundred ton *'Susan Constant',* the forty-ton *'Godspeed'* and - the smallest of the fleet - the twenty-ton *'Discovery'.* All three vessels safely arrived in Virginia on the 20th April 1607 and Jamestown on the 17th May 1607 to establish a new colony on American soil.

After I finished my history lesson, Kipper asked how I knew about the voyage. My reply was very simple. "Easy Kipper, just read the memorial plaque nailed on the river wall."

We were about to return to Lambeth when we sighted an old friend, the bumboat owned by Bill Martin. The *'Henrietta'* was sailing to London, no doubt carrying supplies for ships that would soon be sailing into coastal or continental waters. The *'Henrietta'* furled her sail, which enabled us to get a towline out and allowed us to jump aboard her - no more rowing until London Bridge at least.

Bill Martin glared at Kipper and shouted that he owed him a dented empty tin mug he had stolen on last meeting. Kipper looked embarrassed until Bill started laughing and slapped poor Kipper hard on his back.

"The spinners have done their work well young Maynard", Martin then spoke in an excited tone. He informed me that of late, he had been thinking seriously of Uncle John. He had never believed in the mumbo-jumbo of fate in connection with the three spinners, but he did think fate controlled our lives. Today, fate had brought us together for he had some interesting news for me. Bill continued his tale by explaining that my Uncle's death might not have been an accident. There were rumours about a large smuggling gang operating on the river - not with brandy, whisky, tobacco or women. It was something to do with paper or, to be more precise - paper money. I looked at Bill Martin and laughed, "Surely smugglers make money from tobacco and spirits, not from paper money!"

Bill Martin's expression did not change - he remained deadly serious. "Just consider this young Maynard. What is the weight of one hundred crates of brandy and one hundred barrels of tobacco, and then tell me the weight of ten thousand pounds in paper money?"

I thought about this and quickly realised he was right, although I did not know the answer.

Martin continued, "How much space would you need to stow those crates and barrels in comparison with ten thousand pounds in paper money?" Again, I quickly understood, although the dimensions were not obvious to me either.

Bill Martin was about to ask me how easy was it to conceal paper as opposed to any illicit cargo. I quickly stopped him, shouting, "I get the picture."

This must have been an extremely large gang to smuggle that kind of money into London under the eyes and noses of the authorities. I enquired if the money smugglers had been apprehended or was it still operating, to which my friend exclaimed that to the best of his knowledge, smuggling in every commodity still continued, but not to the extent it was three years ago.

"Why three years ago? I don't understand!" I asked.

Bill's answer was short and sweet, in fact just one word – "Fauntleroy."

The name brought back distant memories, but I didn't recall that much, so Bill filled in the details.

"After seven years working as a clerk in the London bank of Marsh, Sibbald and Company - of which his father was one of the founders - Henry Fauntleroy received a partnership. Eventually the whole business of the bank passed into his hands. In 1824, suspicions were aroused into Fauntleroy dealings and the bank suspended payments. Fauntleroy was arrested and charged with misappropriation of bank funds, and forging trustees' signatures. At his trial, it was rumoured that Fauntleroy had embezzled a quarter of a million pounds which he squandered in debauchery."

Henry Fauntleroy's trial took place at the Old Bailey. With the case against him proved, the man admitted his guilt, although he later pleaded that he had used the misappropriated funds to pay his company's debts, a guilty verdict followed and Fauntleroy was sentenced to death by hanging. Seventeen merchants and bankers testified to his general integrity at the trial. After his conviction, powerful character witnesses came forward. His severe sentence came before judges on two separate occasions, mainly due to points of law. The efforts of his many friends were, however, unavailing, and he was hanged in November 1824. His execution for forgery

31

caused uproar and I think it might be one of the last to take place in this country.

It was rumoured he might have uttered the words – "see you in the Devil's snot-rag soon", but this might have been just an exaggerated story to frighten young children.

I pondered over Bill's story for a few minutes before looking directly into his eyes and asked, "Could it be that insider knowledge regarding the whereabouts of customs men, tidewaiters and preventative officers played a big part in getting so large sum of paper money into the City?"

Bill solemnly replied, "Not possible, I would most certainly say highly probable."

In October, both Kipper and I went to Watermen's Hall with our masters, as did another thirty or so apprentices, hoping to pass our verbal test on river knowledge. With the exception of four lads, we all passed, although I still had other nagging matters on my mind.

Could my uncle's death been prevented? If so, who conspired to kill him?

CHAPTER 4

The spring and summer of 1828

Spring

Having recently passed my two-year examination, I felt much happier about myself. I knew I was now superior to every newly made apprentice and could earn a wage, but I remained inferior to the sublime rank of a freeman. Dedication to the trade would, in due time, reward me. However, nagging doubts remained in my mind regarding the demise of my Uncle John. Was it possible - or as Bill Martin suggested, probable - that his premature death was connected to an evil smuggling syndicate operating in the city of London and the Thames?

I had no idea how to approach the problem. I didn't want to alarm my parents or anyone else connected with the family until I had proof of a conspiracy if my uncle had been murdered. I asked my master, George Wyld, if I might possibly work alongside the tidewaiters at Gravesend for a short time. This would prove important to me when it was my time to be examined for my freedom. I needed to be familiar with the river - especially those lower reaches, as far downstream as Gravesend and Tilbury. It was here that the tidewaiters, like my uncle, waited patiently for incoming vessels to clear customs and to make sure the correct levied duty on the goods they carried was paid.

I planted this thought into my master's mind and suggested that my rowing skills and prowess would be greatly improved if I ever decided to row for Doggett's Coat and Badge.

Uncle John had been most fortunate to compete in the wager. In 1787, lots were drawn at Watermen's Hall to reduce the number of competitors to the agreed six, made up from the ranks of first-year freemen, in compliance with Doggett's wishes. The drawing of lots was deemed the only way to whittle the number of first-year freemen down to the agreed six, although it did not stop some lucky contestant from selling his winning lot to another man. When it was my uncle's year, in excess of two hundred first-year freemen put their names forward to partake in the wager. I am pleased to inform you that my Uncle John finished a courageous runner-up to Benjamin Rawlinson from Southwark.

I suggested to Uncle George that with luck, I could be the first Maynard to win the coveted orange coat and silver badge bequeathed by the famous Irish comedian, Thomas Doggett, over one hundred years ago. Although Uncle George scoffed at the notion, he suddenly recognised the benefits of being the master to a Doggett winner. The accolade of winning would not just be mine; the master would also be heartily congratulated, become a local hero and have drinks bought for him as if he had won the famous historic race.

With the seed sown and nurtured, the flower blossomed into reality; before long, my uncle deemed it his idea, and I had no reason to correct him. After all, as the expression goes, the end justifies the means. I had successfully negotiated a three-month apprentice exchange arrangement, whereby I would gain knowledge from working at Gravesend alongside the tidewaiters.

Bill Martin had assured my family that he would look after me while I resided with his family at West Street, Gravesend; Bill's youngest brother went to Lambeth under the care and guidance of my parents. My only regret was not being with Kipper for three months, but time would pass by quickly.

Accordingly, Uncle George secured a passage for me aboard an empty sailing barge that was sailing back to the farmlands of East Anglia. The captain had orchestrated a short stay at Gravesend to enable me to get ashore at the newly opened Gravesend basin, on the western end of the Thames and Medway canal. On my return to Lambeth, I reckoned that a similar passage in reverse should not prove overly difficult to arrange. I considered the temporary move to Gravesend ideal. Besides learning the lower reaches of the Thames, I should keep my ears open for any gossip and rumours. I was informed that with two ears, two eyes and a mouth, I shouldn't talk too much, abut just listen and watch; perhaps the story should be, as you have two ears and only one mouth, you can hear twice as much as you can talk! Any mention of money smuggling could prove interesting, but I had to be cautious. I was only sixteen and inexperienced.

What should I listen for? Bill told me he would assist as much as he could and suggested that the gang was organised and remained at large despite the loss of Henry Fauntleroy. He thought that by now, they would be tempted to spend their ill-gotten wages. Moreover, he believed that if the gang still roamed the reaches of the Thames, it must have been a family group and not individuals. The head of the family could keep it under his control, whereas individuals might have loose tongues, especially when drunk. Bill mentioned a few families and where they resided, but the names meant nothing to me, even those in the Lambeth area. I thanked Bill for all his help before following him into his West Street residence.

After supper, I checked the list of families Bill had provided to me, but they were just family nicknames – the Bawley boys from Gravesend, the Piglets from Swanscombe, the Captains from Woolwich, the Bread Boys and the Bankers from Bermondsey, and finally, the Priesthood from Southwark. Bill could not offer any names of the families located further upstream of Southwark; but suspected that because of their remoteness, any suspicious activities would be well known to all and sundry. The names made no sense to me, so when Bill returned from loading his bumboat for the next day's voyage, I asked him to translate the list for me.

We went over the names, one by one – 'The Shrimpers' from Gravesend originated from the Bawley boats based at Anchor Cove and Bawley Bay, which were used for the sole purpose of catching shrimp and other small seafood or fish. 'The Piglets' originated from the medieval word for Swanscombe. I knew the old name for a farm was *Combe*, but I didn't understand where the *swan* part came from until Bill put me right - the word *swan* was a corrupted version of the word *sow*, or female pig; hence, Swanscombe becomes pig farm, at one time associated with the area, and thus the word Piglets was born. 'The Captains' derive their name from the Sargent family from Woolwich. The head of the family, an arrogant man, considered himself more important than anyone else on the river, so everyone played a private joke on him, and decided to 'promote' him to the rank of Captain. 'The bread boys' of Bermondsey came about quite simply from the surname 'Baker', very much like how Priesthood originated from the surname 'Abbott', and the 'Bankers' originated from the surname 'Banks'.

I sat with my mouth open, unable to comprehend what Bill Martin had just told me. He laughed and slapped me gently on both cheeks, and said, "Simple, young Mayday." It might appear damn simple to him, but I was completely lost. From all these names, I had to try and find out if any of them had recently spent money, not just a few gold sovereigns, but if they had spent cash on new boats or the purchase of a riverside tavern.

My head was spinning - where do I start? Perhaps the best place to clear my head was in bed. I had an early start the following morning. Bill reassured me he would shake me around five; we'd have breakfast at five-thirty and be out before six.

Before retiring to bed I made just one demand of my host.

"No bloody salmon for the next three months!"

Bill Martin just laughed, whilst his wife Henrietta, not understanding the private joke, looked on in complete puzzlement.

Time for bed.

Summer

Just before six the following morning, I boarded the customs boat that I would be joining - *The Interceptor*, whose second-in-command was Patrick Murphy. All were patiently waiting for the skipper to come back aboard from his briefing at the Fountain, where he would be receiving his orders for the day.

In those days the tidewaiters used various riverside taverns as temporary offices; however, the Fountain seemed the most popular. The crew consisted of six men: the skipper, mate and four men who manned the oars and when required set the sails. It became painfully obvious that the crew didn't like newcomers, especially a sixteen-year-old sprog like me.

Patrick pointed to the four men in turn. "That be Charlie Peek. That low-life scum beside 'im be Christian Bullas. Foreside of them be Joseph and Thomas Masters."

None of the crew acknowledged me, they couldn't be bothered to turn round and look or acknowledge me. From behind me, a voice boomed out, "And I am Michael Laws or Sir to you, boy." The skipper had re-joined the vessel from the Fountain Hotel where he had received his orders for the day. He brushed past me to speak to Murphy. The pair studied the loose sheets of paper held by the skipper's left hand, and at long last, the men shook hands and Laws left Patrick Murphy to declare the orders. With a raised voice, Murphy spoke for all to hear, "Only a couple of worthwhile ships to explore today, lads." The silent response could only be taken as one of abject misery; it appeared the crew enjoyed busier days. The skipper turned to Murphy and enquired who I was, to which the mate ushered me forward and told the captain that I was George Maynard, a two-year lad from Lambeth, on board for a three-month term to learn the trade of being a proper waterman. Laws remained silent, obviously in deep thought. Within a few seconds, he took me to one side, out of earshot of the crew, and enquired if I was related to a friend of his, John Maynard. I politely answered that John was my uncle, being careful to address the captain at all times as "Sir".

Laws appeared perplexed and took his time before continuing the conversation, "Good man, John Maynard...a

39

decent, God-fearing man...sadly missed....knew him well...a good man to cover your arse was John Maynard....heard he died in some kind of accident in London whilst at work." Each phrase ended with a brief period of total silence before he rambled on. The skipper ruffled my hair and told me to keep my head down, blend in with the crowd, never look a dog in the eye and to keep out of his way.

The skipper bellowed out his final order before we let our mooring ropes go. "Lads check your firearms and cutlasses. Keep them dry and safe by your side at all times before we depart. Sorry sprog - no weapon for you. Don't want you accidentally blowing my bloody head off."

The tide still ebbed as we drifted downstream from the canal basin to check on the four vessels anchored off Higham. All waited for the tide to turn, and all four, being much larger than the others that anchored, waited for their pilot to navigate them upstream to their respective points of discharge. No need for us to set sail or get our oars wet, the mate simply adjusted the tiller arm and let the tide do the hard work to bring us safely alongside the nearest vessel – 'The Enterprise.'

Laws and Murphy scrambled up the Jacob's ladder that the ship's crew had left hanging over the side. Once they were safely aboard, Laws shouted down for me to join them, "You ain't going to learn nothing, sprog, by staying in the boat - get topside!"

'The Enterprise' was half-loaded with tea from India; she had previously discharged part of her cargo in the port of

Gibraltar. Once topside, I joined the skipper and Murphy while they studied the ship's manifest. The skipper ordered me to go down into the hold to check on the number of tea-chests, while he and the mate would interview the crew and passengers. "Got to make sure they all are who they say they are." The skipper handed me a scrap of paper on which he had scribbled a figure - 1395 at two guineas custom fee per chest. With that, Laws and Murphy disappeared aft to enter the Captain's quarters, and with the assistance of one crew member, I went down below into the dark hold to start counting. The vessel only had the one hold, so I quickly got to work checking the total number of chests stowed. Fifteen abreast, three high and thirty-one in a line equals 1395 tea-chests. I opened three chests at random to double check the cargo - no problems. Two guineas times 1395 chests equalled £2929.00.

The work was straightforward enough, and nothing seemed improper in the hold. I climbed back on deck to confirm my figures with the skipper and mate, who appeared impressed by the quickness of my work, although I think they wanted to spend more time with the Captain of 'The Enterprise', sipping glasses of Madeira wine.

Laws and Murphy bid their farewells to 'The Enterprise' before disappearing down the rope ladder and back into the customs boat, with me in hot pursuit.

"Next ship!" Murphy shouted to the four bored oarsmen, and off we went to the next ship lying off Higham anchorage.

I sat down on the side benches close to Joseph and Tom Masters, pointed to the north shore and asked, "What about those vessels further downstream on the north shore?" Initially, neither of them wanted to talk, but Thomas grudgingly replied that all of them were coastal traders and therefore exempt from the spying eyes of the customs. I asked about the two vessels ahead of the sailing barges, those bearing the same colours of the French flag, but the opposite way round.

This time, Joe decided to answer my question by telling me that the ships were Dutch, and they had the freedom of the Thames on account of having saved the poor folk of London during the plague of 1665. "Don't know much, do you, sprog?"

I peered over to the north shore as the fleet of sailing barges slowly heaved their anchors up to proceed upstream towards their respective destinations. The majority of the crafts were stackies, or to be more accurate, hay barges. Because of their light draft, they could easily get underway as soon as the tide turned.

The two small Dutch vessels had to wait until the tide had flowed for two or three hours flood before heaving there anchors, while 'The Enterprise' waited for the final hour of the flood tide, before taking her pilot to sail inwards to the East India Dock.

We had cleared all four ships of customs, and collected the required customs duty. Our work was finished, but our responsibilities had not ended. A head-rope was pushed through a link in one of the channel buoys. Charlie Peek, who to date had not uttered a word, yelled out to me to make a bowline and secure the end with a round turn and pin-hitch about our cleat. Evidently, Charlie was testing me; however, after correctly carrying out his orders, no words of encouragement were offered. I thought I detected looks of support from Christian Bullas and the Masters brothers, but nothing more. None of them showed any emotion or gave anything away, except for Charlie, the silver fox on account of his hair colour, who simply grunted.

These Gravesend men - or 'chalkies' as they were known to us upriver watermen - were a sour bunch of men, unlike the river-folk from Lambeth. I was worried if I had made the right choice by coming down to Gravesend to work.

Our twelve-hour shift came to an end at six in evening, and the four oarsmen rowed us back to the canal basin where the night crew took over. I offered a polite goodnight to all of them, which was greeted by a not unexpected silence. As I hurried ashore to return to my lodgings, I thought that they could all go to blazes; as far as I was concerned, the six of them were nothing more than a weak fart in a tornado (not that I had seen a tornado)!

To my utter astonishment, the skipper called out after me, "Good day's work, young Maynard." The crew of 'The Interceptor' followed suit, all with huge stupid grins about their dirty faces. And blow me down! All without exception waved me a goodnight. The damn fools were testing me.

And I did have a good night.

Feeling fully relaxed and confident, I walked the short distance from West Street down to the canal basin, arriving just before six the next morning. As per usual, Tom and Joe Masters were already on their rowing-seats, ready for the day to come. Peek and Bullas were smoking their clay pipes and exchanging shameless jokes regarding ladies of the night with Patrick

43

Murphy. Unlike the previous morning, they all greeted me with a friendly slap on the back, or a slap on the bum administered by Joe Masters, the youngest of the Masters brothers. Skipper Michael Laws joined us shortly after six o'clock, with his list of expected ships which to date only consisted of the two newly anchored vessels down at Higham.

The skipper and mate studied the list and eventually came to an agreement on how the day's work should proceed. Apparently, the two ships at anchor would be attended first while we waited for the arrival of three other vessels, one of which seemed to be of importance to the skipper.

The tide was extremely low; it had not begun to flow, so we had to make use of the oars. Being slack water, Pat Murphy was unsure whether we should come alongside the first ship to be inspected head up and head down. He let 'The Interceptor' drift midstream abreast of the anchored ship, thereby ascertaining if our small boat continued drifting downstream, or as he hoped, found an early sign of a flow. The experiment proved inconclusive, so he ordered the rowers to do as they pleased. Once secure alongside the ship's ladder, the skipper and Murphy, followed by yours truly, scrambled up the ship's side to be greeted by the Captain of the 'Leopard'. The ship was in ballast, that is to say she presently was void of cargo. Her orders were to load a cargo of bagged coal to be discharged at Amsterdam. If the ship was indeed empty, our work aboard would not take too long.

A quick inspection of the hold found the vessel bare, save for the rats. Laws enquired how many crew members were aboard and if any passengers were taking passage on the outward journey. The answer came back quickly - twelve crew and no passengers, although, there might be a couple of passengers

44

joining the ship when they secured in London Dock, but that would come under the jurisdiction of the London Dock customs.

There appeared little to keep us aboard, so we returned aboard our customs boat, ready to inspect the next vessel, which was anchored half a mile downstream. By now, the tide was flowing well, so we rowed close to the shore, making our journey easier on the muscles.

Our boat came alongside the *'Les Trois Freres'*, but alas, no ladder was left out for us to board her. Michael yelled out but got no response from the ship. Murphy checked his paperwork to discover the exact time the ship had anchored.

"She arrived at five this morning skipper."

The *'Trois Freres'* flew the French flag, a nation, up until just over ten years ago, we were at war with. High up the main mast fluttered a plain yellow flag, which I knew would be trouble. I walked aft to point out my discovery to Pat Murphy, who, in turn, pointed out the yellow flag to our skipper.

"Yellow flag fluttering on the main mast means what, Mister Maynard?" he asked of me. I replied, "Disease, Captain." Skipper Michael Laws rubbed his unshaven chin and pondered - was this true? Did the ship carry disease, or was it covering up something their captain didn't want us to investigate? It was obvious by her draft that the *'Trois Freres'* was fully loaded; the paperwork showed the cargo to be a considerable number of barrels of French wine bound for the West India Dock. "We shall have to put the ship under quarantine regulations, Mister Murphy." "Oh shit," murmured Peek, "that means forty days in

45

isolation and no-one to enforce it but us!"

There was nothing further to be done except return to Gravesend, report our findings and leave it to the medical and port authority to come up with an answer. It would have been beneficial to confirm the cause and extent of the sickness, along with the number of individuals affected. However, this would have to wait until access could be gained, and only in the presence of a qualified doctor.

The day had started so well; now, we were left to patrol the yellow flagged ship at a distance. It was decided not to approach the vessel any nearer than two hundred yards. We could see crew members waving and shouting requests for water barrels to be brought out, but we have to ignore the request until our relief crew came on duty, and that would be nine hours away.

The expression – 'pass the buck came to mind'.

With the danger to life, as yet unknown, there was nothing left to be done except to circle around the vessel and warn off any unsuspecting craft that might come too close, and make sure nobody on board left. This had really turned into a shit day, with a further forty days of the stuff to follow.

Had the three spinners contributed to our situation?

The medical authorities decided that Pat Murphy and I should patrol the *'Trois Freres'* in a high-sided waterman's wherry, while the rest of the crew went about their business as normal on '*The Interceptor*'.

To relieve the boredom, Patrick allowed me to practice my rowing skills. We waited until there was a strong ebb tide, which allowed me to row against the tide from a standing start. Pat kept records and timed my progress, which seemed to improve day after day. As the days went by, conversing with Patrick Murphy proved pleasant; he spoke about his wife and family, the dangers of the job and the cold winter weather and working through the night.

I spoke about growing up in Lambeth and the close-knit family life that I had grown accustomed to. Eventually, the conversation drifted to my deceased uncle. It appeared that Pat, as he preferred to be called, had completed several shifts with John Maynard before he returned back to Lambeth. The conversation seemed cordial and relaxed, so I pushed forward by asking if Pat had noticed any changes in my uncle. "What do you mean by changes?" Patrick happily answered. I enquired if my uncle was concerned or worried in any way. He considered the question with great thought and replied that John Maynard did appear concerned, but whatever it was about, he kept it to himself. He said he didn't want to get anyone else involved until he got it right in his own head.

Come on Maynard, another couple of good rowing practices before our shift alongside the dead ship finishes. Unbeknown to us, the '*Trois Freres*' had become a dead ship. While we were happily rowing two hundred yards midstream, four deaths had already been reported in the captain's log.

The forty-day quarantine rule had expired, and our patrolling was deemed unnecessary. However, the harbour authorities still remained hesitant to board the vessel for fear of anyone spreading a disease, which had stricken the crew. Patrick and I had recently re-joined our old crew aboard *'The Interceptor'*, so with a doctor and military orderly aboard, we gently rowed downstream to board the incapacitated ship. We cautiously stood by as the medical team climbed the boarding ladder; once they were both safely aboard, we cast off to a distance of fifty yards into midstream, where we remained, until the doctor shouted that all was clear, and it was alright to come alongside.

Once alongside Michael Laws, Pat Murphy and yours truly went top side to find nine scrawny crewmembers, including the ship's surgeon and the captain standing in a line. The doctor told us that fourteen of the crew had died, including the first and second mates, a cook, an engineer and two cabin boys. They had all succumbed to severe dysentery, probably from the rotten food found in the ship's pantry.

After our shift had finished, I strolled along the river path back to the Three Daws. Solomon Ribbens was still in residence with a smile and welcome hand; however, when he set his eyes on me, he hesitated. "What's the matter Mister Solomon? Cat got your tongue, or has your memory faded? Last time we met, I was in the company of Sir Richard Sharpe. Is the gentleman still in Gravesend, or has he moved on to newer pastures?"

Solomon Ribbens looked perplexed, but he managed a smile and shook my hand, but I honestly think he had forgotten our last forte. Perhaps it was because I was n o w alone as Kipper was in Lambeth. Ribbens had become slow and forgetful, this appearing obvious by serving customers incorrect orders. Bill Martin entered the riverside restaurant and beckoned me to join him. He ordered the drinks - a pint of ale for himself and a glass of lemonade for me - with a plate of crusty bread and fresh shrimps. Ribbens wrote the order on his pad and wondered off to the bar to pull the pint and pour the lemonade, but the poor man forgot the food, which Bill had to repeat.

Once Ribbens had left for the second time, I talked to Bill Martin about my suspicions: Why do we not check the inward-bound coastal ships; why do we treat the Dutch as if they own our river; and why, at times, does a small wherry, with one man aboard, row out to the sailing barges just as they leave the anchorage? The explanation of the Dutch ships was easy for him to explain - the coastal vessels would not be of interest to His Majesty's customs' officers because they only sailed down the coast without straying into International waters. Regarding someone rowing out to the sailing barges, he had no answer, but he was sure it was just a coincidence, nothing more.

I continued to press the point, like a dog with a juicy bone. I had made notes over the past month: the same sailing barge and the same small Bawley boat going out to meet her – that is not a coincidence that is a regular occurrence. Bill wanted to see my note pad and sure enough, the sailing barge, the 'Suffolk Maid', had made seven trips within the last month, and each time the same Bawley boat went out to rendezvous with her. Bill looked up from my list, took a sip of his ale and turned to gaze out of the window. "If your notes are accurate, young Maynard, you could be on to something." Bill was aware that sailing barges occasionally employed the services of an additional licensed hand, but not on a regular basis. Bill took a large gulp of ale before calling out loud where has Solomon Ribbens got to with our bread and shrimps. "No matter", I responded, before pressing on, "is it worth following up?"

"If what you have suggested is true, and I have little reason to doubt you, I wonder where the *'Suffolk Maid'* discharges her cargo." Bill was beginning to get interested, especially when I gave him an answer.

"That's the funny thing, she makes seven voyages upstream, on seven occasions she has someone rowing out to greet her, and this is the point - she returns back down again fully loaded. No cargo had been discharged."

"That doesn't make sense," Bill interrupted. "Precisely," I said. "In addition, according to my figures, the *'Suffolk Maid'* should be back at the anchorage on Wednesday morning for her next pleasure cruise to wherever she goes."

"That's most fortunate," Bill interrupted me again. "I have orders to supply goods upstream to Greenwich next Wednesday. I could follow the bugger upstream to see where she goes."

I reminded Bill about his list of suspects and asked him whether in view of recent information, if we should delete any names off the list. Bill took my note pad and crossed out a few names. "Don't worry about the Piglets or the Captains anymore. The Shrimpers are playing some part in the wretched plot, and I surmise it must be any one from the remaining three names. One of them has thrown their hat in with the Shrimpers. We have to figure out who has decided to work with a team of tosspots! And more importantly, who is pulling the strings."

Bill looked at me after he finished his pint of ale. "You have done well. We always considered the forged money came into the country from France, and that might still be true. The French might have lost the war, but they are still not to be trusted. If we get too much money into our system, it would cause chaos."

"Do you know what our French friends across our English Channel call us? Bloody roast beefs! - And do you know what we call them? Froggies! Apparently, Napoleon started the craze and although he's presently confined in the middle of the Atlantic Ocean on his little island, pissing his bed sheets at night, the little man still tries to pull strings. I think he deserves a bullet in the brain, and not a garrison of English soldiers to wipe his arse. That man will always be trouble."

CHAPTER 5

The Suffolk Maid

In general, the weather during 1828, especially during the summer months could only be described as wet.

It continued to rain as I spotted the sole rower proceeding to the north shore to board the *'Suffolk Maid'*. If they were smuggling they must be extremely stupid, or over confident in continuing their activities. If a sixteen-year-old apprentice could recognise irregularities, why had the port authorities failed to see it? – For now, this remained a mystery. Hopefully, with Bill Martin's bumboat shadowing the *'Suffolk Maid'* I hoped answers would be forthcoming. There was a chance that everything was perfectly legal and above board, but until those questions were answered, it remained a mystery. The only difficulty, as far as I see, was the weather. The rain came down relentlessly, making visibility beyond three hundred yards near impossible.

I worried whether Bill's bumboat would be able to keep in visual contact with the sailing barge, but more importantly where she was going?

It was all in the hands of God, or possibly in the hands of the three spinners. Nothing could be done until Bill Martin returned to Gravesend. My shift finished at six o'clock, and I had not noticed the 'Henrietta' return to her moorings. I prayed nothing had gone wrong, or worse, if Bill had lost sight of his prey due to the atrocious weather, which continued unabated throughout the day. The 'Suffolk Maid' had left her Gravesend anchorage just before seven, with Bill in close pursuit.

With nothing achievable until Bill's return, I made my way to his home at West Street to be greeted by a welcoming mug of strong hot tea served by his wife, or as she allowed me to call her, Henrietta.

Time was passing by, and the 'Henrietta' had not returned. His wife looked anxious as the clock on the table struck ten. I always found the expression – "I'll kill him when he gets home", extremely strange; as Mrs. Martin was not going to murder her husband - she would probably cuddle him to death!

Shortly after eleven, there was a knock on the door. Mrs. Martin asked me to check who it was, and sure enough, it was her wet husband, and sure enough, cuddles and warm kisses continued unabated. Then the scolding began - "Where the hell have you been, I've been worried sick!" Finally, a slap on the cheek and a push meant the ritual was over.

After witnessing the events of the last five minutes, I resolved never to marry.

Bill Martin quickly drained two mugs of tea down his gullet to warm his insides and brought me up to date regarding the day's offerings. He had followed the '*Suffolk Maid*' from Gravesend; although the weather conditions could only be described as horrendous.

At Jenningtree Point, visibility had decreased to less than two hundred yards; at Margaretness, it had reduced to little more than a hundred. Our progress was severely hampered in Woolwich Reach, the cause of which was the relentless driving rain, combined with a strong westerly wind that fought with the incoming tide. Bill explained that he had seldom seen the apocalyptic 'white horses' look so furious, yet at the same time look so beautiful and striking - natural forces working against each other causing a natural disharmony. Both the sailing barge and Bill's craft found scant protection from the unyielding wind as they navigated the huge bend in the river at Greenwich, which as you might recall was our original destination. However, due to the horrific weather conditions, the ship we had to supply had shifted upstream to safer moorings at Pickle Herring Wharf.

I knew Pickle Herring Wharf and its nearby watermen's stairs reasonably well. I tried to picture where the '*Suffolk Maid*' had gone - had she sailed further upstream through the bridges or found a safe haven below London Bridge?

Bill replied in a flash, as if he anticipated what I was about to say, - "Dock Head, or as you might prefer to call it, Saint Saviours Dock."

That was interesting!

St. Saviours Dock (The Neckinger)

Bill looked at me somewhat perplexed, "Why interesting?" To which I responded, "Do you not recall the tale about the Devil and his snot-rag?"

Bill's face went blank.

Bill Martin, I'm ashamed of you," I continued, half-joking and half impatiently. Bill's face remained blank.

"What is the Devil's snot-rag?" I asked - his face remained blank.

This was frustrating!

I gave him a clue, "How would a gentleman say snot-rag?" A light must have flickered inside Bill's brain, as he hesitantly replied, "Handkerchief."

At last I was getting somewhere!

I had to admit to myself that Bill hailed from Gravesend, and probably didn't know too much about the upper reaches. Continuing, I asked him if he knew the right name of the tributary that flowed into the Thames at Dock Head. Bill's face reverted to his blank expression!

Bill exclaimed that he had never entered that small dock-way. He had no reason to enter its bowels; it was a dark, dirty and a totally forbidding place. The warehouses appeared to engulf anyone who ventured into its sanctum sanctorum. Children were fearful of the place because of the tales of demonic monks, devil worshippers, and the gibbets where pirates hanged.

During its long history, the tributary was navigable as far as Bermondsey Abbey. Bill remained unsure of the answer to my question and simply said, "Don't know!"

"Bill Martin, you are a freeman of the Thames and you don't know the names of the various rivers that flow into it."

He jabbered out, "The Quaggy, Roding, Lea, Darenth, Ravensbourne and Cray," but this particular tributary remained a complete mystery to him.

Finally, in desperation, and for my own sanity, I had to tell him. "It's the Neckinger." Bill remained unimpressed – "So what's that to do with Lucifer?"

"The Neckinger means the Devil's handkerchief, remember the snot-rag?" Realisation suddenly flashed on Bill's face. The 'Suffolk Maid' had sailed into the Neckinger, a place synonymous with Henry Fauntleroy's rumoured final words.

"Bloody Hell! You won't catch me going into Saint Saviours, or the Neckinger. If you want to find out where that sailing barge docked, you can do it yourself."

CHAPTER 6

The sinking of the Suffolk Maid

After explaining everything to Michael Laws, he thanked me for my diligence and the thoroughness with which I had collected my evidence. He considered the single rower meeting the *'Suffolk Maid'* and thought it most strange. If it happened on the odd occasion, he wouldn't have had any difficulty explaining the strangeness, but on a regular basis - the same rower meeting the same sailing barge - that certainly needed investigating. What's more, Laws had no theories pertaining to the sailing barge proceeding outward bound, without a straw being discharged, that was suspicious. He enquired when I anticipated the *'Suffolk Maid'* was next due in the Thames.

Assuming my calculations were correct, I told him that the *'Suffolk Maid'* should be back at her anchorage three days from now, just before sunrise, around four-thirty. Our skipper was happy to wait until his shift came on duty to pay her a visit. He knew coastal sailing barges were not normally inspected, but he was sure that he could come up with an excuse for his untimely inspection. I asked about the mysterious rower, to which he told me that he would deal with it.

And deal with it he did!

Patrick Murphy arrived at Bawley Bay, with three marines from the nearby blockhouse, just before six o'clock on Monday the 18th of August. He identified the mystery rower as Simeon Lampwick, who worked for the Shrimpers at Bawley Bay. When confronted with the allegation of suspected smuggling, and being a known felon, he confessed, but only to the lesser charge of moonlighting as a third hand and pocketing the money for himself. Patrick was not convinced by Lampwick's explanation and ordered the marines to hold him in custody until he came off shift. The marines wanted to know on what charge to hold the man. Murphy, normally an affable man, raged at the suspect; his reply was short and to the point – 'smuggling'. With that, the prisoner was restrained and double marched back to the blockhouse and placed under lock and key.

Murphy joined us aboard *'The Interceptor'* to explain what had happened at Bawley Bay and to confirm that the waster, Simeon Lampwick, had been confined within the blockhouse. Laws' plan appeared to be going well: Get rid of the mystery rower, and as I was a decent sculler, I would take his place.

The crew of the *'Suffolk Maid'* neglected to notice a sixteen-year-old boy sculling towards them, instead of Lampwick, a man in his late seventies. It just went to show what being over-confident could do.

I came alongside the *'Suffolk Maid'* but her two crewmembers immediately became suspicious of my presence and enquired the whereabouts of their arranged third hand. I informed the churlish pair that Lampwick was sick and had asked me to deputise. Sadly, this answer proving unsatisfactory, they reckoned they could do without me, impolitely telling me to clear-off. With those words echoing in my ears, I swiftly departed in case I aroused further suspicion. Once back aboard *'The Interceptor'* I reported my misfortune to Captain Laws.

He simply responded by saying, "Understandable, I suppose".

Michael looked troubled, deep in thought. I offered my apologies for being unable to board the sailing barge, but Laws waved away my apology, saying the fault wasn't mine, and that he had already devised another plan. "We mustn't allow that stackie to leave the anchorage." That was the easy part of the hastily amended plan. The crew of the *'Suffolk Maid'* were detained and brought ashore in irons, protesting their innocence. Murphy, together with Tom and Joe Masters, took command of the barge. Once the anchor had been heaved aboard, they sailed inwards to the Neckinger. The only flaw in the plan was that no-one had any idea of the berth within the Neckinger they should come alongside. The former crew were exceptionally uncooperative regarding this matter.

This time the *'Interceptor'* was the shadowing vessel, and Murphy made sure he kept close to her stern. At East Lane barge moorings the *'Suffolk Maid'* drifted with the tide before navigating to port to enter the mouth of the Neckinger.

What was Laws' plan? I knew he must have confided in Murphy, but without the prior knowledge of a destination, entering the Neckinger could prove disastrous.

The *'Suffolk Maid,'* with the *'Interceptor,'* close astern, proceeded up the Thames to East Lane barge moorings. At this point, the *'Suffolk Maid'* swung to port to enter the Neckinger. They had not gone much further than two hundred yards into the tributary when she suddenly veered hard to starboard and smashed her bow into a warehouse by Jacob's Island. With the sailing barge holed below the waterline, she was taking in water fast. Murphy and the brothers had safely scrambled ashore, but the fate of the *'Suffolk Maid'* was in the hands of the three spinners, or most likely, the grip of the slurry and brown water that now engulfed her.

We waited to see who might come to the barge's rescue. Suddenly, it became painfully apparent – too many well-meaning rescuers!

We lied to those ashore, telling them that the barge crew were somewhere in the murky water, possibly drowning. Laws had to think quickly to mask our presence. Needless to say, Pat, Joe and Tom were safely ashore concealed within the warehouses. The Neckinger wasn't called the Venice of drains for nothing. The tributary was one of the most contaminated waterways in London, and prone to deadly diseases.

The *'Suffolk Maid'* was taking in water fast and in danger of turning on her side. The force of nature had taken over when the plans of men had seemingly gone violently wrong. Without warning, a small boat with two occupants rowed down from the upper reaches of the dock and attempted to board the stricken barge. Saving the cargo seemed an impossible task, but the two men appeared uninterested in the hay or anything that might have been hidden within it. They went directly to the rudder of the *'Suffolk Maid"* now visible as she lay partially on her side. A watertight box

63

had been concealed around her rudder, and that appeared their sole desire - to retrieve the box as soon as possible.

Within seconds the box was freed from her rudder, and the small boat retreated up into the bowels of the Neckinger.

The *'Suffolk Maid'* had turned over on her side, athwart of the channel, completely blocking the Neckinger. Her cargo of hay had spilled into the already blackened water, causing the dock to take on the appearance of a rain sodden wheat field. The dock was in a total mess and un-navigable. The *Interceptor* was unable to proceed further into the dock, so Laws decided to stay close-by at Horselydown stairs - the upper side of Saint Saviour's Dock - to await the arrival of Murphy and the Masters brothers. With the tide ebbing, the lumpy, sodden hay had begun to drift out into the river, causing widespread navigational problems. What a calamity! No one could have foreseen this! We had only one thing on our side - prolonged summertime daylight - but plenty against us. Why had the sailing barge veered off course? Did this have anything to do with the concealed box about her rudder? But more important to us, where was Murphy, Tom and Joe?

Laws regularly checked his pocket-watch; at his last glance, the clock showed nine, and there was still no sign of the missing men. A deeply concerned Charlie Peek and Michael Laws went ashore to search the back alleys and warehouses within the Neckinger. Only Christian remained with me aboard the *'Interceptor'*. Finally, a cry from the shore alerted us from our morbid thoughts. Laws shouted for us to come ashore to help. What we found had a lasting impression on me for the rest of my life. Standing alongside Joe and Tom, I could see Charlie in a total state of desperation; all three were in a state of severe shock. Lying on the dirty, wet cobbles, I noticed, what appeared to me as a pile of sacks. Whatever it was had been covered by more sacks. Upon closer inspection, I recoiled when the sacks were drawn aside to reveal the body of poor Patrick Murphy - throat slashed from ear to ear. The liquid on the cobbles was not just dirty water puddles; Murphy was lying in his sticky, red blood. Without success, Michael tried to calm us all down. Can you imagine the sheer horror of the scene? Our good mate and colleague had been murdered and left to bleed out to die alone in a dirty alleyway, engulfed by the shadowy warehouses that had scared the life out of William Martin a few days earlier.

Without any police to help, we carried Patrick's lifeless body back to the *'Interceptor'*, and covered his motionless remains with as much respect and reverence as our present circumstances allowed.

Michael Laws, standing aft, muttered an apt prayer to our fallen comrade before casting off to sail back to Gravesend. The spinners had cut one of the threads of life, and Patrick Murphy had been the victim, cast adrift and allowed to fall from the wicked world in which he lived and worked.

We all hoped that wherever his soul had gone, it had to be a much better place than this sinful world from where he departed.

CHAPTER 7

Interrogation

Patrick's funeral had been a sad affair. Saint George's Church at Gravesend was completely full. Afterwards, a private ceremony took place, about his grave, at the local cemetery. It had been agreed that his widow and two children along with four brothers and one sister would attend the committal, with his former crew mates there as an honour guard about the grave. Amanda Murphy's children couldn't contain themselves and had to be taken home by their aunt.

At the Three Daws, we celebrated Pat's life. Solomon Ribbens and his wife did Murphy's family proud – the food and drink flowed all afternoon and well into the evening; all paid for by the tidewaiters of Gravesend and London. At long last, the guests dispersed, leaving his widow, Michael Laws, Charlie Peek, and Christian Bullas, Tom and Joe Masters and me to contemplate the horrendous events that had taken place at the Neckinger. I had never met Pat's wife, but it was obvious the couple, who had recently celebrated eighteen years of marriage, remained besotted with each other.

Although the binding rules prevented me from entering a

public house, I received a dispensation from my master and Watermen's Hall, allowing me to attend the funeral and wake on the strict understanding that no alcohol passed my lips.

I had been deeply concerned about whether my pursuit of justice for my uncle's death may have brought about Patrick's horrific slaying. If I hadn't been so keen in tracking down any leads pertaining to my uncle's so-called accident, Pat Murphy might still be alive; however, Michael told me to wipe that idiotic notion from my head. With the Gravesend part of the smuggling ring in jail, and three men in custody within the cells of the blockhouse awaiting interrogation, we could now make considerable progress regarding the murderous upriver part of the gang.

So far, the three men had not divulged any worthwhile information, but it was still early days. Michael informed us that a team of specialist interrogators would be questioning the three men shortly. Perhaps they could get answers where we had failed.

The atmosphere on board the *Interceptor* during our final shift together was extremely tense. We had lost a popular friend, and what was worse, the remaining crew were to be uprooted and scattered to the four winds, or somewhere within the Limehouse or Wapping areas. We were only going through the motions – even Michael Laws had lost his enthusiasm. Christian and Charles remained positively solemn all day, and the normally talkative brothers remained silent. We had five ships to inspect that last day, all of which were routinely cleared. All five were in ballast to load outbound cargoes; therefore, we left the dock authorities to sort out and clear the paperwork prior to sailing.

With the shift complete, we rowed back, in total silence

68

to the canal basin where William Martin was cheerfully waving at us. Bill greeted us with the biggest smile I have ever seen, it was spread right across his ruddy face. At least someone was happy that Saturday afternoon. Bill took our head line, which he secured around the nearest bollard before scurrying aft to place our stern rope through an iron ring, sliding a metal toggle through the eye to make fast. The forward and aft spring moorings were the last ropes to be secured. With the oars safely stowed and our sail neatly folded and tied beneath the rowing benches, I bailed out any surplus river water, which completed our daily ritual. The *Interceptor* was now ready to be handed over to the next and final shift. On Monday, the tidewaiters were to be dispersed within the various docks. Fresh lodging had to be found, and families were going to be displaced.

Laws looked thoroughly dejected and downcast, as he had all day, but urgently wanted to know why Bill Martin was so cheerful. "The bastards are singing like canaries. Those intelligence officers called in from Horse Guards had convinced Lampwick to turn King's evidence. The bastard has not stopped talking since."

What's more, the two rogues from the *Suffolk Maid,* not wanting to have their necks snapped by any hangman's noose, have willingly agreed to testify and tell all – they even named the smugglers at Saint Saviours Dock. They are being rounded-up and imprisoned as we speak.'

Laws desperately wanted to know who the intelligence officers were and to shake their hands for their splendid work.

"It turns out we know one of them – they have invited us to share their good fortune at the Fountain."

When we arrived at the Fountain Hotel, Bill Martin guided us to the upper floor, to a table occupied by one man. The table had been strategically placed by the side of a huge bay window, and the table was overflowing with food and drink. The window offered unspoilt views of Gravesend Reach.

Bill Martin introduced Lord David Hill, fresh from Horse Guards,' Lord Hill was a man in his early sixties; clean shaven with a tanned, weather-beaten, scarred face. He was well dressed, wearing civilian clothes and leather riding boots, although, it seemed clear to me he had seen much military action.

We were all hankering to shake the hands of the men who had extracted a confession from Lampwick and the two despicable rascals arrested aboard the *Suffolk Maid.* Laws noticed Lord Hill's hand was grazed and scabbed with fresh blood, but informed him that a certain amount of pressure had to be exerted on Lampwick to justify his method of extracting a confession. His Lordship assured us all the blood on his hand was not his.

I looked around to see if anyone else stood close-by. Bill Martin had told us that we were familiar with one of the interrogators; all I saw was one man, of whom I was unfamiliar.

"Good afternoon young Maynard," the voice called to me, as it steadily climbed the stairs behind me. It was Sir Richard Sharpe, who looked splendid in his army uniform. "Good to see you again young Maynard!" To which I stuttered, "and...you...sir."

Sir Richard wore the full-dress uniform of a Colonel of the ninety-fifth rifle brigade, famous for their exploits at Waterloo.

For a while, he looked much larger and impressive than I remembered. While the rest of the crew stood back in awe, unsure how they should greet a man with such a lofted title, Sir Richard Sharpe came right up to me and gave me a manly hug.

Now that our party was complete, Lord Hill described the grilling of the prisoners but thankfully omitted all of the unpleasantness. Once Lampwick was made fully aware by Lord Hill that Murphy had been unlawfully killed, he immediately capitulated. Smuggling was one thing, but murder was something quite different – it carried the death penalty.

It didn't take too long for Lampwick to yield; self-preservation was a wonderful thing, and not unsurprisingly, the two men aboard the *Suffolk Maid* agreed with Lampwick. The questioning revealed that the Abbot family, or as you call them, the Priesthood from Southwark, were in charge of the London end of the business. At present, no individual has admitted to the murder of Patrick Murphy. In fact, every member of the gang supplied just one name.

Laws impatiently demanded the name of the killer, however once revealed he recoiled in disbelief.

"Fauntleroy."

We all started to prattle among ourselves, making listening impossible. Sir Richard appealed for calm. He agreed with Laws that the name Fauntleroy was most certainly a red-herring. The forger had been hanged for his crimes four years earlier – that was definite. The unfounded rumours that circulated regarding a silver tube being placed down his windpipe in an

71

attempt to cheat death were just that – unfounded!

"What I do know," continued Sir Richard "is that on the thirtieth day of November 1824, Henry Fauntleroy went to his maker, with the largest crowd ever to be assembled at a public execution outside Newgate Prison to witness his final dance. Every available window and rooftop capable of glimpsing the gallows was occupied."

"When Fauntleroy was lowered from the gallows he was definitely dead – and that is an undisputed fact. I know, because I was there."

Laws wanted to know if Henry Fauntleroy had any siblings capable of avenging his death. Sir Richard was unsure, but Lord Hill was checking on this train of thought.

Sir Richard knew Fauntleroy's father had died prior to the execution. He was aware of a brother called John and a sister, Elizabeth, but their whereabouts remained unknown. There had been reports that the siblings had departed England for America to escape the shame and humiliation.

Laws and the rest of us looked utterly confused and bewildered. If Fauntleroy had died dangling on the end of a rope outside Newgate Jail, who was this individual masquerading as Fauntleroy?

Sir Richard simply said, "Lord David Hill, you and I have to find this impostor. Clearly he thought Henry Fauntleroy was nothing but a vile charlatan instilling fear and panic into the minds of the gullible. Whatever the truth, although this loathsome killer had been repeatedly named as Fauntleroy, that couldn't be true!"

It appeared that the Abbott family never met face-to-face with the man posing as Fauntleroy. They received their instructions from notes left under designated marked empty beer barrels in the backyard of the Jamaica Tavern.

Laws knew the Jamaica Tavern at Southwark from his younger days. Oliver Cromwell had frequented it during his commonwealth era, and if his knowledge was correct, the licensee was a man called Thomas Cross. Lord Hill confirmed that Cross was the landlord and confirmed he was clear of all involvements and irregular activities at the tavern.

Michael Laws enquired if Lord Hill or Sir Richard knew what might have been secured around the rudder of the doomed sailing barge.

Sir Richard considered the question and surmised that the box contained printing plates – the type used for printing forged paper money.

What he said next surprised us all.

"The ultimate counterfeiter isn't a crook. He's an artist!"

"Be that as it may – the man is a frenzied murderer."

Lord Hill, who had not spoken for some time, asked just

73

one question, "How do we catch a ghost?"

How indeed!

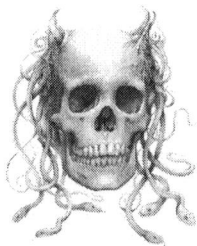

CHAPTER 8

Good news - bad news

With my three-month exchange at Gravesend complete, I returned home to Lambeth and my parents. Mother kept talking about the fine manners of Bill Martin's younger brother, while father expounded on his virtues. He considered the youngster to be the best apprentice he ever had the privilege to teach, but I couldn't tell if he was joking when he told me that Bill's brother was a far better sculler than I was. I looked him square in the face just before he exploded into laughter, and a friendly rough-and-tumble game followed.

I hadn't told my parents about the murder of Murphy or my suspicions regarding that the death of my uncle had been anything other than pure accident. I kept everything to myself, but these secrets weighed heavily on my mind. Getting a good night's sleep proved difficult. Nightmares regularly roamed through the crevices of my brain. I was constantly reminded of Patrick Murphy, picturing his body lying on the filthy cobbles of the alleyways of the Neckinger; his head nigh-on separate from his shoulders. There were times when his lifeless head spoke to me – it moved, it turned, and it blamed me for his death. Murphy's head kept telling me, "I shouldn't be dead."

Mother regularly entered the bedroom I shared with my brothers to make sure I was not hurting myself and to discover the cause of my shouting and blaspheming in my sleep. The ghostly visions seldom went away – if anything, they got worse. I thought my nightmares would cease if the killer was arrested. If this was achieved, I hoped Patrick could rest in peace.

Time passed without any fresh clues coming to the fore pertaining to the man pretending to be Fauntleroy. I hadn't heard from Lord David Hill or Sir Richard Sharpe in more than four months. It appeared as if the killer had gone to ground, like a fox eluding the hounds. I tried desperately hard to concentrate on my apprenticeship and in particular my rowing skills - I practised daily. Sunlight was my salvation, but as the night always followed the day, I dreaded the hidden horrors that awaited me from the shadows. There were plenty of times I literally forced myself to stay awake, but this only brought on hallucinations due to deprivation of sleep. I was in a mess.

Christmas came and went, but it held no joy for me. Presents were exchanged, and the family celebrated the festive season, but I continued to battle the terrors within my head. Patrick wouldn't leave me alone.

Early January brought me a small chink of light. It came when an elderly gentleman knocked on my parents' front door on the specific orders of Lord Hill.

A gentleman introduced himself to my mother as John Crawford, aide to Lord Hill and friend to Richard Sharpe. When Crawford knocked on the door of our terraced dwelling in Lambeth

High Street, he seemed to block out the sunlight due to his massive frame. John Crawford was exceptionally tall – in excess of six foot six inches, and as wide as he was tall. He ambled into my parents' house, with the aid of a walking stick. I could tell mother was scared witless and I was slightly fearful of the man. Luckily father had already departed and was probably, at this very moment, rowing his first customers of the day across the Thames.

Mother, reassured that our visitor meant her no harm, offered to make tea, which Crawford gracefully accepted. He needed her to leave the room to enable him to have private conversation with me. Crawford asked if I knew of a small lighterage company who named their lighters after African animals, to which I answered, "yes, the Abbott's."

Crawford then enquired if I recalled any of the names of the lighters – "*Lion, Gazelle, Mongoose* plus a few others." I told Crawford that the Abbott family owned about a dozen barges. Crawford mentioned the name of another animal and asked, "Is the *Jaguar* part of their fleet?"

I nodded in agreement just as mother re-entered the room. I wondered where the conversation was going. "Sorry to trouble you ma'am," Crawford addressed her with an impressive smile, and asked, "Would you have a slice of cake or a biscuit to accompany the tea ma'am?"

Mother left the room in a huff and headed back whence she came. Once she was out of earshot, John Crawford revealed that the '*Jaguar*' was the barge that had collided with my uncle's wherry. "It was owned by the Abbott family – The Priesthood."

77

If this was true, surely the whole family could be arrested and charged with murder, or at the very least of being complicit to murder. Crawford explained that this would be problematic, as the entire Abbott family were in jail on the day of the murder. The family had been charged with being drunk and disorderly; they had a cast-iron alibi handed to them by the authorities.

Crawford replied straight away as he perceived the look of utter despair upon my face. Although what he said made sense, it was that strange I had never considered the scenario before.

"Whoever steered that barge into the path of your uncle's boat must have known how to navigate such a craft." That made perfect sense – a lighterman, or bargeman or maybe a fellow freeman of the Thames had murdered Uncle John and probably murdered Patrick Murphy.

Why had I not considered this before?

Crawford continued with his reasoning, "There cannot be that many men who have mastered the skilful art of forgery and skilfully navigate a barge." The problem was that Crawford didn't know anyone with those combined talents, and neither did I.

I enquired if Crawford was absolutely certain that every member of the Abbott family had been locked up when my uncle was killed. Crawford looked apologetic as he answered, "I can assure you the whole family was attending a wedding when a fight broke out between various members of the Abbott family. All of them were rounded up by the local constabulary and subsequently incarcerated within Southwark Police Station; they were definitely there during the time your uncle was killed. I have the names and addresses of every family member once we threw them out from the cells. You can take my word for it, every member of the Abbott family spent the night under lock and key."

I tried to make sense of what Mister Crawford had told me. First, the Abbott family were up to their rotten scrawny necks in a smuggling racket that involved Fauntleroy, or someone who copied the man's methods. Second, and more important to me, this same man was probably responsible for the death of my uncle. Third, Patrick Murphy had been murdered by this same person – and he might be a fellow licensed freeman or bargeman. I tried to work out some kind of common thread, but failed to find one. Perhaps those three spinners would reveal the wretch to me, either by chance or design, but I highly doubted it.

John Crawford had revealed all he knew and was about to depart when, thinking aloud, he said, "We could leave some juicy bait for him, like the greedy shit and contemptible individual he is. He might be tempted to take the bait as long as what was on offer couldn't be refused."

"What would tempt him," I asked. It was plain that Crawford had not thought that part through, but he knew two friends who might have an idea – Lord Hill and Sir Richard Sharpe.

He left looking slightly happier than when he arrived, and promised to keep in contact. John Crawford was very much a gentleman, and as I believed him to be a gentleman, they invariably kept their word.

You have to remember, I was only a youth, approaching seventeen, and seventeen-year-old lads have little in the way of patience. When I shared this knowledge with Kipper, he looked dumber than me when it came down to understanding strategy or baiting a hook with a juicy worm. The bait couldn't be money, as the man simply printed his own – a forger – he was that rich that money meant nothing to him. What was he after? I tried to recall a saying from my father told me concerning the evils of money. I desperately tried to remember his words, but it wasn't easy remembering sayings when I was a ten-year-old boy.

"Money is the worst currency that ever grew among mankind. It sacks cities and drives men from their homes; it teaches and corrupts the worthiest minds to rotate."

Kipper came up with one of his silly sayings, the only problem with his sayings is that they sometimes made sense. Out of the mouths of babes he offered this great advice: "Greed is so destructive, in time it will destroy everything." That made sense; Fauntleroy simply had to print money to overload it into the monetary system. If there was too much money floating around within the system, the country would eventually go bust.

Was this the aim of the counterfeiter? Did he want too much money in circulation to push the country to the brink of bankruptcy? Who would benefit if the country were insolvent? That particular question I wrote down on paper to ask Sir Richard Sharpe or Lord David Hill next time we met – it might make sense to them.

It certainly didn't make any sense to me, but I was only a lad, while all three of them were powerful individuals within the establishment.

Mother must have thought we boys were growing up at last. She thought Kipper and I had been chatting about catching girls. Men and boys were the master hunter-gatherers – we had to devise a fool proof method for trapping the female nest-maker. However our trap was to capture a killer, a trap from which he couldn't escape.

Sir Richard had to tempt the bastard to come out of the shadows. If he was our killer, we needed him to accept the bait as a matter of honour to his ego and make him think if he won the challenge, he would become the undoubted winner.

To Kipper and me, our strategy was straightforward. All it required was for Lord Hill, Sir Richard Sharpe, and John Crawford to iron-out any rough edges, forcing the devil to break cover. The plan might work, unless the spinners had other ideas!

We didn't have to wait too long. Four days later, outside the Custom House at Lower Thames Street, we spotted our three friends – so far, the three spinners hadn't interfered. We disclosed our plan, which, after careful thought, all three considered it worthy of examination. Sir Richard even broke into song as he sauntered inside the Custom House; *The Harp of Love* from James Fennimore-Cooper's latest book entitled *The Spy*.

Lord Hill and John Crawford abruptly stopped on the steps leading up to the Custom House.

"Richard," Lord Hill shouted to attract Sharpe's attention. "We have just had a thought. What if the killer has French sympathies?"

"Whatever gave you that idea? An interesting theory and one we have not previously considered!" Sharpe was now feigning as he considered Lord Hill's proclamation, an assumption shared by John Crawford. Sharpe repeated his question this time trying to keep a straight face, "What made you think of a French connection?"

Crawford explained that the jolly song that Richard had just struggled to sing came from a musical play written by James Fennimore-Cooper, but Sir Richard tried to remain flabbergasted. He continued his thespian act by telling his friends that he failed to see any connection between *The Harp of Love* and a French conspiracy. Crawford was getting frustrated and asked Richard if he knew the title of Cooper's book in which the song came. It appeared to Crawford from Sir Richard's expression that he had no idea, although he recalled the song had American overtures – Yankee Doodle-Doo comes to mind. Crawford was getting angry with Sharpe: "you may have come up through the ranks, Richard, but show some common sense. The damn tune is from the musical play entitled *The Spy*."

"So it is!" Sharpe retorted. Richard had been mocking Crawford and Hill for the past ten minutes, and what made it worse was when Richard ended his play-acting by saying, "Why hadn't he considered that?"

"You bloody deceitful bastard, Richard!"

Richard Sharpe elucidated, "I might be a bastard, but at least I duped you two dandies."

Sharpe, like most of England, had worried that the revolution in France would find its way across the channel. Why it didn't happen was pure luck, certainly – the populace was ripe for revolution. George III was bloody mad, and his heir led such a lavish life-style that he was trying, single-handedly, to bankrupt the country with his incessant spending. He was also doing his best to increase the population of England by fathering illegitimate children. His heavy drinking, together with rumours of an addiction to laudanum, made him an easy target for ridicule.

Sharpe paused for breath, asking if he should continue.

"No need," Crawford intervened, his weight, near-blindness, increasing waist size and severe gout making it near impossible for the King to sign state documents. Even his doctors informed me the King was wasting away, all of which had been well documented.

Hill decided to put his two pennies in by saying that the last time he saw the King he had become obese, and found the slightest of movement extremely difficult.

Sharpe considered his assumptions right regarding French tentacles spreading unabated across the channel to take root on English soil. If Napoleon had beaten us at Waterloo, half the gentry of England would have invitations to Madame Guillotine.

Perhaps the three spinners had a hand in our destiny.

King George IV did his best to inspire revolt. The principles of revolution were prevalent within our society – cultural, social, financial, and economical revolt. Perhaps our one redeeming feature was our stable government; this had already undergone significant changes during the time of Cromwell.

It was when two young lads provoked me by wondering what would happen if the winner took all that I immediately thought of revolution. If too much money was in circulation, it would cause massive inflation. And inflation only hits the poorest, thereby creating a recipe for revolution.

Richard then spelled out what was now painfully obvious – he believed that revolution was the danger we all faced should our killer get his own way.

"Fauntleroy was just a greedy bugger; this adversary is attempting to stir up social unrest. And we still do not know who he is. If Thomas Paine were alive, I might have considered him our adversary, but he died in America near-on twenty years ago."

CHAPTER 9

Mother Flanagan's

Funny, since last meeting Sir Richard, Lord Hill and John Crawford, I felt I had regained some of my own self-respect. My nightmares had all but ceased, and I was feeling positive for the first time since Murphy's murder. It might have been due to being home in Lambeth, and, of course, being with my friend James Kipper. We trained together, as both of us had decided to put our names forward for the Coat and Badge wager bequeathed by the famous Irish comedian, Thomas Doggett.

In past years, it was common knowledge that those who wore the famous orange coat and silver arm badge were made for life. They could put their names forward to join the Royal watermen corps, to protect our sovereign when he journeyed on the Thames.

Everything in London, especially on the river, remained quiet. Nothing out of the ordinary happened, life continued as normal until early March. And then the unthinkable happened.

Rumours quickly spread concerning the Prime Minister of England, His Grace the Duke of Wellington had accepted a challenge to duel with the Earl of Winchelsea at Battersea Fields. Initially, no one knew the cause of the strife between the two men. Father always told me that barmaids should never repeat conversations they overheard in public houses, and watermen should never repeat anything overheard in their wherries. If barmaids had big mouths, then watermen had bigger ones. Being only a two-year man, there were times I had overheard the most embarrassing of tales. Some were clearly rubbish, but others were of a more delicate nature. The idea of the Duke of Wellington fighting a duel seemed ridiculous; however, the stories persisted to such a degree that bookmakers began taking hefty wagers on the outcome.

Father explained to me that the Duke was opposed to duelling to such an extent that, as Commander-in-Chief in the Peninsular War against France, he invoked article 114 of the military code to prevent duelling many times.

Was it true, or was it an exaggerated fairy story? Was the Duke about to accept a challenge from the Earl of Winchelsea to fight a duel? I considered the matter ludicrous – how could two grown men want to fight each other over some petty disagreement? If I had a difference with Kipper, we would go out to the backyard and square-up to one another. But I very much doubted that either of us would actually want to finish the other off.

Stories circulated daily, until it became clear that the disagreement concerned an Irish problem. The Duke, being Anglo-Irish being born in Dublin, was in favour of Irish Emancipation, whereas Winchelsea was fervently against it. I had difficulty pronouncing the word, let alone understanding its meaning. But Uncle George Wyld explained that it was something to do with freeing the Irish. I still didn't understand what was going on, as the Irish were already free to roam wherever they pleased. I had many Irish friends – some worked on the Thames as watermen and lightermen, and they became freemen of the river. The Irish labourers sweated and aided in the creation of the new docks. If this was the world of adult behaviour, then I was happy to remain a youth, even though I would be leaving my teenage years behind next year. I only had a few years of my apprenticeship left to serve before hopefully becoming a freeman.

I wondered what Sir Richard and his two companions thought about the Duke fighting a duel. All three were in the army, all three had been under the command of the Duke, and all three remained loyal to their country, if not wholly to their King – all three were loyal Englishmen. I had not seen any of them since our last chance meeting outside the Custom House.

Besides the duel and the freeing of the Irish, other stories were circulating, one of which I wholeheartedly supported. Adults, I thought, sometimes made the correct decisions. Mister Robert Peel, our Home Secretary, intended to establish a full-time, professional, and centrally organised police force for the Greater London area. It was to be known as the Metropolitan Police. If this newly organised force had been established the previous year, perhaps Patrick Murphy might still be alive, and the wretched murderer of my Uncle John might have been under lock and key. However, we cannot turn the clock back. If the lock was rusty, no matter how good the key, it wouldn't secure the prison door. Likewise, if the lock was new and the key rusty, we had the same problem. What was required was a new police – an adequately staffed police force – last year's force of a mere four hundred was inadequate for our needs.

I wondered if the three reports were connected. Had the spinners been at work?

First, the Prime Minster, the Iron-Duke, was against Emancipation. Then he changed his mind. Then the Earl of Winchelsea challenged the Duke to a duel – a man who was solidly against duelling, and finally, Robert Peel planned to establish a new police force.

Coincidence or fate?

Coincidence left to man? Or fate in the hands of the spinners of destiny?

On the 1st of April, father read an article in the Penny Post newspaper confirming the duel had taken place at Battersea. However, the report stated the following:-

"A duel took place on Saturday morning in Battersea-Fields, between His Grace the Duke of Wellington and the Earl of Winchelsea. It is reported the duel originated in a letter written by the Earl on Friday night to the Duke, on a subject connected with the important question now in progress through Parliament. Sir H. Hardinge was the Duke's second, and the Earl of Falmouth was Lord Winchelsea's, who, instead of returning the Duke's fire, discharged his pistol in the air. His Grace was seen riding through Horse Guards at six o'clock on Saturday morning, and returned to Downing Street at eight o'clock."

Father considered the newspaper report and looked at me in amazement. "Why did Winchelsea fire his pistol skyward?" Mother, who had received a good education from the church, had been listening to our conversation. She answered father by saying the reason a person fires his pistol in the air had French connections, derived from the French word *'delope"*– meaning to throwaway or discard.

I stared at mother in disbelief, unable to comprehend what she had just said – a French connection?

Mother looked at me slightly puzzled and told me to stop gawking. I didn't know how to respond. I hadn't mentioned to my parents anything about Patrick Murphy, Uncle John, or the army intelligence officers. Instead, I told her I was unaware she spoke French. To this, she replied that she read about two American politicians, one of whom is thought to have deloped by firing his pistol over his opponent's head. She couldn't recall the names of the politicians involved but remembered one of the names had an association with a Scottish town. She just guessed at the answer – Angus, Aaron, Hamilton, or Dumbarton. To which I jokingly replied, "Dumbarton – was he a deaf-mute?'"

Mother rarely punished any of her children, but I got a clip about the ear on that day, and probably deserved it.

Perhaps I was looking for answers that weren't there, or maybe the question hadn't yet been asked. More likely, our sinister fiend had yet to show his hand and was now keeping safe within the dark shadows of his lair. If Sir Richard Sharpe, Crawford, or Hill had devised a plan, there was no sign of it. The barmaids and watermen remained silent, no rumours or gossip had been spread. If there was a tale, the barmaids would hear about it first, then the watermen, and then every living soul in London would be aware of it.

Perhaps the brute had flown back to France or wherever he laid his hat at night.

I decided to put my faith in the hands of the experts – the so-called spies and intelligence officers who kept us safe at night.

The year seemed to pass exceptionally slowly. Thomas Maynard, no relation to me, was hanged for forgery, and the last of the *Bounty* mutineers, John Adams, had died on the Pitcairn Islands.

We celebrated Christmas, and a new year dawned. A new horizon and a new year – what had 1830 in store for us? King George died – the King is dead; and his brother William took the throne – Long live the King. Joseph Grantham, one of Peel's new police force officers, was accidently killed whilst attempting to break up a fight between two brawling drunks. The jury decided the officer's death was justifiable homicide; probably due to the fact that the new police force was, as yet, not universally popular.

What did attract my attention was news coming out of the mouths of barmaids, which quickly spread to the streets of London. In France, there were reports of another revolution, albeit lasting only three days, but it resulted in the overthrow of the French Bourbon monarch, Charles. The French King and his son had fled to England. If revolution was in the air and spread unchecked like a wildfire across Europe it might spell trouble for England.

Italy, Poland, Greece, Belgium, and the Netherlands experienced revolution in one form or another. Thankfully, the United Kingdom remained unscathed for the moment. Had our tormentor left his burrow to wreak havoc across Europe, spreading his wicked lies and expanding fear in his wake? Perhaps the three spinners were gazing down towards England with kindness and compassion. Or was it Great Britain's turn next? Sir Richard, Crawford, and Hill must have had their suspicious. If so, what were they doing about it?

Fortune favours the brave, as His Grace the Duke of Wellington once told his antecedent Yorkshire regiment. If mainland Europe was in turmoil, England would soon follow.

As a young man of twenty, I had no idea what was happening. My old skipper one told me to keep my head down and blend in with the crowd. As a waterman, I could keep my head down, and as I was one of in excess of 30,000, I could easily blend in with the crowd. That is precisely what I did – I kept my head down and blended in, watching, listening, and learning.

Customers, for whatever reason, always ignored the servant; they always talked freely as if we were invisible as if they were completely alone, and without a care in the world. I watched, listened and learnt. I learnt about two newly arrived French vessels, void of cargo, *Le Grande* and the *Royal Fuetan*. Both ships safely anchored at Gravesend waiting for pilots, bound for London Docks. Why would empty French ships come to London? There's no profit in transporting thin air! Perhaps they were smuggling someone into London, or did someone need to urgently leave London. Whatever the reason, I needed to find my old skipper, Michael Laws.

Whenever I had a fare going downstream below-bridge, I scouted for any of my old friends and my skipper, but the river frontage in the East End of London was a hive of activity, leaving me to smell a fart in a windstorm!

In August 1830, my master, George Wyld, rowed with me conveying six tea merchants from Paris Gardens downstream to the old Hermitage causeway. George needed to carry-out repairs to his wherry and suggested I get a quick bite to eat at Mother Flanagan's coffee house. The coffee house was a mere fifty yards from the top of the causeway, which enabled me to keep an eye on the wherry and a watchful eye for my former tidewaiters. As I walked towards Flanagan's, I encountered a disabled army veteran sitting by a shop doorway with a placard with the words "spare a penny for an old soldier" about his neck. The scruffy old man was attempting to keep warm with a well-worn faded redcoat and patched trousers, all of which required washing. I noticed his dirty toes protruding from his boots, and by his side, his old battered hat was strategically

93

positioned with a couple of farthings nestling within. It was very sad when these men, who had put their lives at risk, turned to street-begging for their next meal or mug of gin. Sadly, I had nothing to offer the old soldier except a cheerful smile and a good morning. Suddenly the old man whistled an old army song, the words of which he doubtless didn't know. The tune was happy enough, with a familiar jolly chorus, but the whistling was so ghastly I had to quickly walk by.

Returning to Uncle George, I told him of my unexpected meeting. He thought it highly unusual if Mother Flanagan allowed anyone to beg near her establishment, as they normally drove customers away. When we turned back to look for the old soldier, he had gone – no doubt Mother Flanagan had won her war. When Wellington's army drifted back to England, tales of horrific bloodshed were often told – whole companies had been obliterated by cannon, cavalry, or musket fire. The slaughter of the French at the hands of Field-Marshall Blucher was unrivalled. This was understandable, as Blucher had a score to settle with Napoleon, and settle it he did.

On the 18th of June 1815, the butcher's bill exceeded 50,000 dead or wounded with 8,000 French prisoners taken, and Napoleon had escaped the battlefield intact, only to surrender to Captain Maitland aboard *HMS Bellerophon* the following month

All those men who fought for King and country came back home to England's green fields to find no prospect of work, and little in the way of opportunity, they had no money. I could see why Robert Peel had planned his new police force; the honourable soldiers applied to become upholders of the law, and the rest simply drifted into crime. One-time comrades became today's enemies.

The six tea merchants requested our services a few days later, and asked to be conveyed from the Paris Gardens stairs downstream to the old causeway at Hermitage. However this time, once safely ashore, they wanted my uncle to remain alongside the causeway, as they intended to return within the hour. With nothing to do except wait, I wandered off in the direction of Mother Flanagan's. To my utter astonishment, the old soldier again sat begging for coppers, just as he had two days earlier. I put a halfpenny inside his battered hat, wished him well and walked on. Yet again, he tried to whistle his song, and yet again he made a terrible mess of it.

I peered through the grimy windows of Flanagan's coffeehouse and, to my pleasant surprise I recognised Tom and Joe Masters sitting at a nearby table. Without thinking, I entered Flanagan's and made my way towards the brothers, when a huge buxom woman barred my path.

That was my first encounter with Mother Flanagan.

After the brothers had vouched for me, I sat down beside them to catch up on all the news. It appeared that Charlie Peek had moved to Deptford to work within the Royal Dockyard. Christian Bullas reckoned his was too old to be uprooted and remained at Gravesend. Tom and Joe, being both unmarried, had moved to Wapping to work alongside the skipper, all three being integrated into new shifts and working in Saint Katharine's Dock.

Tom promised to pass on my regards to Michael, and I left Flanagan's happy in the knowledge I had found three additional friends working ashore for the dock customs. All that remained was to try and find Sir Richard and pass on my knowledge regarding the two empty French ships soon to arrive in London Docks.

I didn't have to wait too long before I saw Sir Richard. Actually, what I should say is that he found me. George Wyld explained that a messenger from Watermen's Hall had demanded I attend the Hall the following Monday morning at nine o'clock precisely. My uncle thought I was in trouble or maybe marked for service aboard a man-of-war. England was always at war with one nation or another and always needed experienced seamen or, failing that, Thames watermen to serve on a blockading ship or a vessel seeking out French or American privateers.

I entered the Hall just after eight-thirty and waited in the hallway before proceeding to the clerk's office. My heart was pumping with extreme trepidation, not knowing what to expect. I had only attended the Hall twice before – once when I was bound, and second when they examined me for my two-year certificate. As the clerk's office was void of any other person except me, it seemed safe to assume there wouldn't be a transfer to His Majesty's navy. Henry Humpherus, the assistant clerk, ushered me into the parlour room and closed the door behind me, leaving me completely alone with my thoughts and anxieties.

I waited for what seemed an eternity, shuffling from one foot to another. The parlour clock ticked, ticked, ticked in rhythm with my discomfort; my heart ached within my chest with worry – had a customer complained?

Another agonising five or six minutes passed before the door opened behind. My limbs felt heavy, my throat went dry, and my head throbbed – what had I done wrong?

"Don't worry lad," Henry Humpherus whispered behind me, "the officer who wants to speak to you is running late. Please take a seat."

This was like pulling teeth at the dentist. I just wanted to get it over with, whatever today had in store for me. This waiting was unfair. I sat down in a convenient seat close to the door. Another few minutes passed when I heard heavy footsteps in the hallway outside. This waiting was driving me mad. It was easy to imagine how a convicted felon felt whilst waiting for the hangman to pull the lever to the trapdoor. The parlour door opened, and the new arrival commenced whistling out of tune. Who had summoned the filthy beggar to Watermen's Hall? I was certain I had been polite to the old soldier; I even put a coin inside his hat. I quickly turned and looked straight into the eyes of Sir Richard Sharpe.

Should I laugh or cry at the sight of Sir Richard? My original reaction was one of anger, which quickly subsided to feeling great relief which ended up with me blurting out incomprehensible words. Or, to be accurate, I mumbled – my brain had gone blank. I wanted to call him all the foul names under the stars, but I had to remain calm. How could I call a Knight of the Realm a thoughtless wicked bastard for making me feel so ill? What came out of my mouth instead was just a series of one word questions – what, who, you? I felt like a stupid boy again, tricked by an older relative.

Sharpe got straight down to business, wanting to know what I was up to, sneaking around London Dock. He went on talking, not bothering to wait for answers. He continued his sermon by explaining that he had been on surveillance outside the dock entrance checking on strangers entering Flanagan's coffee-house. His lecture commenced in his normal self-assured voice, but as he progressed, his tone grew louder and insistent. Finally, he banged his fist on the table, making me jump out of my chair, as he ordered me to explain why I was present at a location of such great importance to the country.

I felt like a scolded schoolboy waiting for a ruler to come crashing down on my arse. This was unfair; all I had done was try to find my old friends and bring myself up to date with their news.

Sir Richard had aggravated me, done me wrong. A response was called for, and I had to defend myself, as I knew I had done nothing wrong.

My initial anger towards him calmed down. He seemed most interested when I mentioned two French ships had recently anchored at Gravesend.

"Both empty in ballast, you say, completely empty, both French? Interesting, very interesting."

It was easy to see he was contemplating various trains of thought and he was formulating something inside his head.

"The names of the French ships were what again?" he asked in a friendlier tone.

I replied, "*Le Grande* and the *Royal Fuetan*."

Richard started to reply, but it appeared he was talking to himself, "The first ship has a common enough name for a French merchant ship. However, the *Royal Fuetan* conjures up something different in my head." He explained the name *Fuetan* had Spanish origins. "And do not be distracted by the *Royal* prefix. That could just be a diversion to confuse us."

Sir Richard took out a sheet of paper from his waistcoat pocket and wrote down the letters: 'R O Y A L F U E T A N'. Sir Richard began rearranging the letters. "A-U-N-T. No that won't do. . ." He was talking to himself again. L-E-T-A-N – again he discarded the letters, screwed up the paper into a tight ball and threw it on the floor. A smile broadened on his face. Instead of scolding me, he now called himself certain names I prefer not to quote.

'R   O   Y   A   L   F   U   E   T   A   N'

Showing me these letters he had written down, he asked what I could see.

"Nothing," I replied.

He again pushed to paper in front of me. He was excited and laughing as if he had found buried treasure in his backyard. "Look again, young Maynard! It is very easy once you see through the deception."

I checked the letters again, but still couldn't recognise whatever his Lordship was seeing.

He wrote the letters down again, this time much bigger.

'R   O   Y   A   L   F   U   E   T   A   N'

Underneath, he wrote the name Fauntleroy. "Do you not see, George? If you rearrange the letters into a different order, the name *Royal Fuetan* becomes Fauntleroy. I believe this style of writing to be called an anagram."

Sir Richard carried-on laughing louder by the second. Henry Humpherus came back into the parlour to ascertain the cause of the jollity. He probably thought the well-dressed intelligence officer from Horse Guards had gone mad. But noticing that I was not in any danger from his outbursts, he decided to retire.

Richard Sharpe was confident he knew the name of the vessel that would bring a killer into to London or assist his escape. Whatever it was, he hoped to be one step ahead of the man.

I made my apology to Sir Richard and Henry Humpherus, explaining that I had an afternoon and evening's work ahead of me. As I left the building, I could still hear Richard Sharpe laughing uncontrollably.

CHAPTER 10

Saint Katharine's Dock

The *Le Grande* docked alongside the eastern wall of Saint Katharine's Dock at ten on the morning of 29th September. The preventive officers, as they preferred calling themselves as opposed to tidewaiters, were waiting on the quayside to board the ship, making sure nothing was in the hold or concealed anywhere else about the ship. Her Captain cooperated fully with the customs officers sent aboard. The paperwork and manifest papers being in order, the ship cleared customs within the hour. A mandatory inspection of the crew's quarters revealed a partially drained bottle of brandy, accidently procured from the bond locker. The customs men cordially shook the French Captain's hand, informing him that once her cargo of bagged wheat had been loaded, they would return to clear the ship for her outward voyage. The manifest told them no new crewmembers or passengers would join the vessel prior to sailing.

At eleven-thirty, the *Royal Fuetan* entered the lock gates; once the river pilot stepped ashore, the dock pilot boarded to assist in her navigational needs to bring the ship alongside the northern wall of Saint Katharine's. Michael Laws and his team waited to board her once she had been secured alongside the quay. With her gangway lowered, she was ready to receive the customs men, her London agent and the Captain's wife. No one noticed an old soldier begging for morsels by the lock side. It was extremely easy to not notice something that was right in front of your eyes, thus confirming my first introduction to my old skipper aboard *The Interceptor* – keep your head down and blend in.

The agent carried bundles of papers and numerous documents stating that her sole cargo would be household furnishings belonging to French Royalist sympathisers, who had fled France for the safety of England prior to the revolution and the Napoleonic wars. It seemed strange that the exiles had waited fifteen years after Napoleon's surrender before returning home to France. The paperwork showed twelve families joining the *Royal Fuetan,* thirty-six individuals plus the Captain's wife, who waited patiently on the quay alongside Laws. Besides the crew, that meant fifty-one individuals to check prior to sailing.

Richard Sharpe was happy sitting in squalid conditions besides horse dung by the wicket gate, which led to the dock masters office. Observing Sir Richard was John Crawford, suitably camouflaged in his stevedore's garb. I had joined the mooring party, blending in. Having completed those duties, we gathered in a nearby hut to keep out of the rain. The rain started to fall as the ship moored, and it steadily worsened; by the time the gangway was lowered, the rain fell in torrents. I swear, if we hadn't been standing on solid ground, we would have all been drowned. I turned to check on Sir Richard in his beggar's clothes – he was no longer laughing, but I was, as was Crawford.

After Michael Laws, accompanied by Tom and Joe Masters and a few other officers, had boarded the *Royal Fuetan* to carry out their duties, there was little to be achieved, unless the murderer was already on board the ship. However, the betting was on the felon making his escape back to France. The customs officers remained on board for nearly three hours, searching every nook and cranny. Eventually, the officers came ashore; by the expressions on their faces, it was clear she held no hidden secrets. Crawford sauntered over to me, expressing his opinion that the ship was too clean – and that was highly unusual.

It was good to meet up with my former skipper. I shook his hand warmly and nodded my acknowledgements to Tom and Joe. The skipper looked gloomy and cheerless. However, when I told him to be exceptionally diligent and careful when searching for a stowaway on her departure, he told me I had misinterpreted his mood. It had nothing to do with finding the loathsome killer; his sour notions had come about due to missing his time afloat at Gravesend – meeting, searching and clearing everything that moved in and out of London's highway. Michael continued with his thinking, "Mark my words, just as the bridges crossing the Thames will prove your demise, the building of the docks will prove mine. Anyone can climb aboard a ship to clear its paperwork; it takes years of experience to navigate the likes of *'The Interceptor'* within Gravesend Reach. Next year, or the year after, our services will no longer be required. They will get students to replace us – no offence young Maynard."

"None taken skip," I replied.

All of us, except for the old soldier begging for pennies, ambled over to the dock masters office to dry out. The rain had not stopped. Crawford peered out of the window to check on Richard and said, "The bloody fool just sits there, nothing will happen until the passengers or the cargo are loaded. Damn his eyes. He won't be told, he thinks he knows better than Hill or me." *He probably does*, but I kept my thoughts to myself. Richard Sharpe had been in many battles during his long life, and barring a few visible scares and a slight limp, he still looked remarkably fit for his age. He might be stubborn, but he wasn't a fool.

The ship's agent, accompanied by the Captain's wife, boarded the *Royal Fuetan* after the customs officers disembarked. Other than that, nothing out of the ordinary occurred. Crawford surmised vigilance would be required tomorrow morning when the French exiles boarded with their worldly possessions.

Back at the Custom House that evening, after Sharpe changed out of his rags, dried and made himself presentable, a debriefing took place. Besides Sharpe and Crawford, Michael Laws and Lord Hill attended, as did I – a lowly, twenty-year-old, scruffy apprentice in the company of his superiors, just like the motto of the Watermen's Company. Crawford announced that four of his men were watching the *Royal Fuetan* as he spoke.

Laws confirmed the deployment of additional custom officers within the dock, and Lord Hill, who considered himself a bit of a legend in the art of espionage, would personally inspect every ounce of furniture brought through the dock gates destined for the ship; although, what he meant was his undercover Peelers would inspect the cargo.

Something had to happen tomorrow; if not, it would be up to Crawford to explain the excessive overtime payments to his staff as well as the custom officers. Sharpe made a joke declaring it was always down to the paymaster-general to win wars.

Before sunrise, Sharpe was back in place, sitting beside a cart full of dung ready to be transported upriver to Chelsea to fertilise their plants. As usual, no one noticed the filthy beggar, in fact, most gave him a wide berth. How he managed to prevent himself from vomiting was beyond me – the dung cart had a steady supply of new horseshit piled into it daily.

Perhaps Sharpe was the legend and not Hill. Meanwhile, Crawford and Hill enjoyed a hearty breakfast before assembling in the dock masters office just after eight o'clock. Michael Laws, along with Tom and Joe Masters, stayed close-by, and two gangs of stevedores patiently waited for the first of the cargo. Normally, one gang would prove adequate, but some of Robert Peel's Bobbies had swelled the ranks.

We waited and waited, no cargo had arrived at the quayside for loading. The stevedores and peelers were getting impatient for action, and it was nearly mid-day, although no one on board the *Royal Fuetan* appeared concerned. Patience was wearing thin, so Laws decided to enquire where the passengers and cargo bound for the vessel had got to, explaining that two gangs were on standby on the quayside waiting to get going. The French Captain reverted to not understanding English, of which he understood very well yesterday. Crawford, who spoke excellent French, joined Laws in the Captain's cabin and threatened to withdraw the dockworkers labour until the following day, but even this threat failed to have the desired effect. Crawford began to smell a rat. Something was wrong, something was very wrong.

Crawford left the comforts of the cabin to shout orders to the waiting stevedores. "You can all go home, I am placing this ship under arrest," and with that both he and Laws disembarked the vessel via the gangway, marching back to the dock masters office. Lord Hill joined the men in an intense argument. Crawford was convinced, as was Laws, that the French Captain was messing them about. Lord Hill agreed and questioned if their reasoning was wrong. Could we all have got it so wrong? Maybe it was the *Le Grande* that needed investigating, and maybe Sharpe got it wrong.

It was finally resolved to send one gang to the eastern quay where the *Le Grande* laid. All agreed to this until a knock on the window abruptly ended the discussion. Sir Richard had been listening intensely to the debate and reminded those inside the room that Napoleon's downfall was splitting his force; if they wanted history to repeat itself, he told them, "Go ahead, split your force. But you are wrong." With that, he repositioned himself, un-noticed alongside the dung cart, content that he had averted a huge error of judgment.

To be on the safe side, Crawford ordered one of his spies to check on the *Le Grande* and report back if anything seemed unforeseen. It didn't take too long for the man to reappear, confirming all was quiet on the east quay. Crawford, Hill and Laws looked confused, while Sharpe looked smug sitting alongside his pile of horseshit.

Without stevedores waiting by the *Royal Fuetan*, all was at a standstill, until the London agent returned to the dock masters office late in the afternoon. He requested the dock master to order a dock and river pilot, as soon as convenient, because the exiled passengers and their belongings were making their way to Dover. From Dover, it would be considerably quicker for them to get back home. The agent apologised for all the problems caused and paid the appropriate fees accordingly. It was Sharpe's turn to express his surprise, and another rat to smell.

Crawford, Hill, Laws and Sharpe sat around the small table inside the dock masters office in total silence. What had they all missed? Something had happened before their eyes, and they all missed it. Laws turned to Crawford telling him that nothing had happened, no passengers, no cargo and no bloody Fauntleroy impostor. This was true. Who was playing tricks or were the spinners playing games?

We better release the ship, order the pilot and let her sail at first light – damn her.

The ship wasn't damned, but could the spinners be playing games? They proved that nobody notices an old soldier begging for pennies, just as nobody noticed what was in plain sight before their eyes.

A scruffy, twenty-year-old, waterman apprentice put them right – even Sir Richard Sharpe. However, that only happened after the *Royal Fuetan* had sailed.

Nobody could be bothered to ask the apprentice.

CHAPTER 11

A Cornish red herring

Sharpe knew his brawling days were over, but he still considered his thinking skills well honed, and he could still take care of himself in a tight situation. Crawford was the spy master and Hill, the so-called legend, was the enforcer. Sharpe just got things done, but yesterday things hadn't been done – what a bloody mess!

Crawford double checked all the overtime payments for the customs men and peelers, and it added up to a tidy sum; now he had to justify the expense to Horse Guards, who in turn had to substantiate the excessive disbursements to the Prime Minister. What a damn mess, he thought.

Lord Hill ate breakfast in peace at his home in Park Lane – he didn't have to answer to anyone. He was in the clear, he just took orders and made sure they were carried through, although yesterday was a bloody mess; even though the plan had not been his, if he was honest, he would have done exactly the same thing. And if so, he wouldn't have enjoyed his breakfast quite as much as he did – he would have mumbled "what a mess" too.

Laws, on the other hand, was completely exonerated and clear of all responsibilities. He probably would have been more assertive with the French Captain – he knew instinctively the man was stalling for time but couldn't think why. What was he up to? It seemed as though the man didn't want a single passenger to embark or any cargo loaded – but why? Upon reflection, Michael Laws considered yesterday a shambles.

George Maynard sat with his siblings at the breakfast table, waiting for his mother and sister to serve the first meal of the day. Father had eaten earlier to check on his wherries for the day to come. George, and his elder brother Henry, who would soon become a freeman, would join their father at Lambeth stairs to tidy his boats. George had remained silent about his movements the day before and his recent interview at Watermen's Hall. He simply told his father a white-lie, telling him it was a mistake in identity, just a mix up with a George Henry Maynard from Stepney – wrong family.

George Maynard was lost in thought; a point not lost on his older brother who mocked him about being in love and teased him about young Sarah Harle who had recently moved nearby. All this was furthest from his mind. George was mulling over the events of yesterday, and he too couldn't make sense of the proceedings that had unfolded before his eyes. It was like peering at a rainbow, right there in front of you, ever so tangible, but impossible to touch. Finally, he dismissed everything from his head because work beckoned.

Sir Richard walked the short distance from his lodgings to Horse Guards, where he met Hill and Crawford. The three men sat in silence, waiting for someone to make the first excuse. Eventually,

Sir Richard spoke, imparting to his companions that yesterday was a complete nonsense of monumental proportions. This was true, and neither Crawford nor Hill could declare the contrary. In his mind, Richard was convinced that they had all overlooked something that was in plain view. He therefore proposed to gather everyone who was at the quayside the day before to an emergency meeting – let them all have their say. Someone must have seen something that the rest of us missed. Crawford and Hill agreed but considered the exercise a waste of time. If a spy and the enforcer had failed to notice the conjuring trick, no one would have noticed it. Richard looked at his friends and without flinching stated, "Arrogant people are insecure, and often repel others." Crawford and Hill looked at each other before focusing on Sharpe in amazement; they had not fully understood the wit aimed at both of them.

Time was of the essence, as the *Royal Fuetan* would be sailing from Saint Katharine's Dock at mid-day, leaving just two hours to get everyone together in one room. Sharpe reiterated, "Everyone who had been at the quayside the previous day, including Laws and his customs officers, the mooring crew, the stevedores, the dock master, the London agent, the peelers, together with Crawford, Hill and me." Crawford meekly enquired if and why George Maynard should be invited, to which Sharpe angrily responded, "If he was there yesterday, I want him here today. Of course he should be here!" Messengers were quickly sent out to gather the thirty men and one apprentice.

When I arrived at the meeting, I had to apologise for my lateness due to work commitments. I had been conveying a family from Lambeth to Westminster when I received the message. Crawford and Hill offered me angry stares, but Sir Richard appeared accommodating, as I sat down towards the rear of the room. It was like being back at school with the assembled crowd raising their hands in the air to speak. The throng mumbled their way through utter nonsense for over an hour; it was apparent no new leads were being explored. Sir Richard left his place at the top table and started to pace about the room. He always told me he did his best thinking on his feet.

As he walked past me, he bent down to enquire why I was the last to arrive, to which I explained I was in the middle of the Thames, off Westminster, when I received the message from a fellow waterman. Continuing, I told him I would have been quicker had I not been waiting for the wife of the family – she found walking down the causeway rather disconcerting.

Sir Richard stood erect and smiled. Of course, he remarked, we all forgot about the waiting wife; so far, no one had mentioned her. She had been waiting alongside the agent for the ship to dock. Sharpe waved to the agent, requesting him to join him back at the top table for a private chat. Crawford, Hill and Laws had no idea what was going on until the private conversation had finished; then Sharpe stood, placed both hands on the table to stabilise himself and enquired whether anyone present remembered the Captain's wife – her facial description, how old she was, the colour of her hair, her height, even what she was wearing. No one recalled these things as nobody was scrutinising her – all eyes were on the *Royal Fuetan* and her Captain. She was standing in front of us all but stayed invisible, just like a smelly, old beggar.

Sir Richard considered the woman an important part of the puzzle until I put my hand in the air. My words echoed around the room, causing most to stare at me in disbelief. "Was it a woman? Or was it a man disguised as a woman – a man wearing woman's clothing!"

113

Silence, utter silence. Not a soul in the room could answer the question, not even Crawford the spy master or Lord Hill the enforcer, both remained tight lipped and sullen.

"Men, it appears a young apprentice has greater alertness about him than all of you put together. We now have a clue to explore, let's get going and put our theory to the test." Sharpe asked Michael Laws for an estimated position of the *Fuetan*, to which the tidewaiter replied, "Erith." I could not ascertain if Sharpe deliberately missed out the word *Royal* from the ships name, or if he considered the vessel to no longer be royal, but just a fugitive to be investigated and searched.

Speed was of the essence. Four horses were brought, and within minutes, Sharpe, Crawford, Hill and Laws were galloping off on their way to Gravesend. The ship had to change pilots off Terrace Pier, the river pilot had to get off and the channel pilot board. If the *Fuetan* was the lower side of Gravesend and in the estuary, all hopes would be dashed. There was a possibility of a small boat intercepting the ship to bring a passenger ashore, but Sharpe was adamant – whoever or whatever the passenger might be, they were probably not the wife of the Captain and still aboard, taking passage to France and outside our authority. There was nothing the rest of us could do but sit and wait for news.

That news came shortly after five in the afternoon. Crawford had sent a telegram; however, it didn't make too much sense. It simply said, *'Ship impounded, under arrest, anchored at Higham Bight, no female aboard, correct number of crew, all of whom accounted for.'*

We all imagined Sharpe's colourful language as this unfolded.

Laws had instructed the Admiralty Marshall's office to nail a writ on the mast of the *Royal Fuetan*, thereby preventing the vessel from continuing her voyage, although everyone knew Crawford was pulling the strings. The reason her arrest was given as customs irregularities, thus avoiding any diplomatic problems between France and Great Britain; however, the arrest warrant could only be enforced for forty-eight hours before the ship had to be released or charges brought. Armed marines were strategically stationed about the vessel to prevent anybody from absconding, and the Captain was placed under armed-guard within his cabin. With the apprehension of the vessel, Crawford and Hill were able to commence the interviews of every person aboard, not that they expected anyone to freely offer information. They could tell that the crew, with the exception of the officers, had been thoroughly intimidated.

Crawford and Hill, accompanied by two royal marines, started the interrogations. They had twelve crew, an engineer, two mates and the captain to question before night fall, and if required, a further day tomorrow before being released or charged.

The Captain, who miraculously regained his knowledge of the English language, protested in the strongest terms, demanding to be told on what charges the ship was under arrest. Hill stated rules this and that, subsection a-z, paragraph God knows what of the customs code of conduction – in other words, he had no idea if there was a code of conduct. Hill was bullshitting as normal. The French captain insisted on a representative of his government being present, which was immediately turned down on the grounds that His

115

Majesty's Customs and Excise superseded the requirements to have a lawyer in attendance, let alone an official from a foreign power – more bullshit. Eventually the interview began. The captain sat bolt upright with folded arms and was tight lipped throughout the interview, save for continually repeating *"je n'ai rien à dire!"*

Hill was bored with the lack of progress, and to prevent him from losing his temper, he ordered the marines to escort the captain back to his cabin and return with the second mate. The interrogations continued with Crawford asking the questions, because Lord Hill had little to no knowledge of the French language. The second mate entered the cabin, followed in turn by the twelve seamen, the engineer and finally the first mate. Lord Hill turned to Crawford, stating that the morning was a complete waste of time – we learnt nothing. Crawford replied confirming no information had been forthcoming, but he was convinced that one of those questioned was their man. "Let's eat, David."

The questioning continued after lunch, but this time Crawford tried to sound more officious. There seemed a slightly better response to his questions this time, but with no new leads, Crawford was getting frustrated.

Lord Hill wanted to try his special method of grilling the crew, but Crawford decided to hold back for the time being – he didn't want a diplomatic row with the French to overshadow his investigations. "Let's try a different tack," he explained to Lord Hill, "no heavy stuff; let it be our turn to be tricky." Hill appeared deflated; his confidence had temporarily deserted him.

Forget about the officers, my hunch is that one of the sailors is our man. One by one, the seamen returned for a second quizzing. As each one arrived, he warned them to be careful when sitting as the chair had become unsteady. The first eight looked back in confusion, not understanding English. The ninth man entered with the same cordial warning offered. The seaman thanked Crawford for his concern before sitting, his accent being unmistakably Cornish. Realising his slip of the tongue, he tried to leave the cabin but the two marines barred his exit. Crawford looked at Lord Hill and smiled. "I think the game is up, don't you Hill?"

Being a cautious individual, Crawford considered questioning the remaining three seamen, to which Hill agreed and said, "It will only take a matter of minutes." Satisfied they had taken every precaution after the final seamen passed Crawford's language detection, both men were confident they had apprehended the felon, although why a Cornishman should be a crewmember aboard a French ship was beyond both men. The grilling of the crew had proved hard and taken its toll on Crawford and Hill; both men knew they were not getting any younger – they both needed a break.

After supper, the Cornishman returned for his third questioning session. This time, Lord Hill asked the questions by first demanding his name. Henry Thomas Trevaliant was the reply. Hill quickly regained his confidence and received answers to his questions without hesitation, until the tricky question relating to Murphy's demise cropped up, to which Trevaliant loudly protested his innocence – and that he could prove it.

Trevaliant told his inquisitors that his father was from Brixham in Cornwall and his mother French; hence, he spoke both languages fluently. "I had been languishing in a French prison awaiting trial for smuggling when an Englishman asked me if I wanted to earn some quick money. I told him, who wouldn't? Whatever his status, he had contacts, and my release was granted the following morning, and hence my arrival aboard the *Royal Fuetan*." Crawford enquired how long Trevaliant had been in France prior to his prison stay, and the answer brought combined groans from Crawford and Hill – five years.

Trevaliant wanted to know why we spoke of murder as he thought smuggling was the reason behind the vessel's detention. Crawford ignored Trevaliant's remark; instead, he enquired if a woman had boarded the ship at Saint Katharine's Dock. Trevaliant wasn't too sure because he had been below deck when the ship berthed; he told them he hadn't seen a woman since his release from prison.

Hill resumed the conversation by inquiring if any sailor had recently gone missing, to which Trevaliant answered, "One sailor had been taken ill with a fever, never saw him again. I presume he died." Hill released the Cornishman back into the company of his fellow seamen. Once he left, Crawford spoke. "We have been well and truly bamboozled David. We must get to the bottom of this riddle before nightfall tomorrow, or Horse Guards will bloody well crucify us."

Crawford confirmed he would be sending a message to one of his agents in France to check Trevaliant's story – best to double check and take nothing for granted.

"Let's get some sleep and rethink the situation tomorrow morning."

118

Therefore bed it was, not that sleeping in bunks was quite like sleeping on a comfortable feather mattress and a duck down pillow. Both Hill and Crawford were in foul moods the following morning, due to the lack of a good night's sleep and severe back pain.

CHAPTER 12

Misery and despair

A spectacular white Christmas preceded the first great fog that descended over the river in the first month of 1830. In the very first week of the year, many lives were lost due to the intensity of the fog. As the days passed, the weather grew steadily worse with a significant frost covering the freezing water of the Thames. While the common folk enjoyed the frost fair on the Thames, we, the watermen, the lightermen, and the dock workers, failed to earn a living. And, no earnings meant no food on the table. In contrast, the summer months of 1830 were exceptionally warm and dry. However, the frost came early with the late ushering in of autumn, accompanied by freezing rain. The heavy torrents hit London quite hard, causing widespread flooding; we encountered fourteen inches of rain in one single day. The river-folk of London considered the two years, 1830 and 1831, to be exceptionally unkind, bringing nothing but misery, despair, and destitution.

My own family tried their best to continue working despite the severe weather. But, cruel conditions, on many days, made it impossible to work. Not a soul, apart from the occasional frolickers, ventured onto the Thames, except on the lower reaches below Deptford, where clear water flowed.

The frost fairs enabled some to make money, especially the raucous crowd who were drawn like moths to the flame. Fairground proprietors and publicans erected huge fuddling tents for the beer sellers, who earned a living serving purl, a mixture of gin and wormwood wine. Homemade ales, oxen roasted over open fires, hot chestnuts, and gingerbread were in abundance for those that had the money to buy them.

The people of London revelled. In some way, it did feel good to witness the celebrations; we were no longer at war, and it was a time of peace. The Allied forces had beaten the monster out of France fifteen years earlier, and the introduction of the railways meant riches for some and greater poverty for most. The accelerated growth of London exacerbated the class divide. The wealthier classes immigrated to the suburbs, while the poor remained to inhabit the inner-city slums.

It was a time to forget one's problems, even if it was only for a week. The problems never truly disappeared, they came back to haunt the same people. Just about everyone enjoyed the attractions that the fairground had to offer in addition to the circus that boasted of having wild animals. There was even an elephant upon the ice. It was only the river-folk that looked depressed, and why wouldn't we? We were out of work and were starving.

I hadn't received any news from Crawford or Hill, who were busy interrogating suspects aboard the *Royal Fuetan*. And, Sir Richard had departed on another assignment. This left me to contemplate if the killer had been apprehended and placed in chains, or if the parasite had managed to vanish into thin air.

Rowing for Doggett's Coat and Badge was furthest from my mind. Of course, Kipper and I always kept a lookout to eke out a living. But, times were extreme for most of us at the waterage fraternity. It was impossible to overhaul and renovate our wherries—the frost made sure of that. But, surely the frost couldn't last forever. It was just that after the frost, the rain started to fall. It seemed to rain continuously throughout the year, with violent thunder storms lighting up London's skyline in the month of August.

On the 4th of August, 1831, my eldest brother, Henry, rowed for the annually contested Doggett's Coat and Badge race. The race should have been held on the first day of August. But, that being a Sunday, the race was scheduled for the next day. However, the crowded state of the river due to the opening of the New London Bridge meant the race had to be postponed until Wednesday. My whole family was there to support and cheer for Henry. He finished a creditable runner-up behind the race winner – Robert Oliver from Deptford. Father must have bought every available copy of the Morning Chronicle, and he kept on reading the report while emphatically stating that Henry would have won had it not been for one reason or another. The newspaper made an interesting read, and I will retell the report to you.

"Hitherto the young watermen have contested for the Livery and Silver Badge, bequeathed by Doggett, the comedian, on the first of August; but in consequence of his Majesty having expressed his intention of opening the New London Bridge on that day, the match was postponed to yesterday. It will be in the recollection of our readers, that Doggett, the celebrated comedian, bequeathed a sum of money for a coat and badge, to be rowed for annually by young watermen, in honour of the happy accession of the family of his present Majesty to the throne of these realms. The match was confined to youths, whose apprenticeship had expired

between the first of August in one year and the first of August of the succeeding one, and about thirty watermen, coming under the above restriction, entered their names at Watermen's Hall to compete for the prizes. The following however, drew lots for the privilege of rowing;-

Henry Colcomb of Queenhithe
J.Carmarthy of King James's Stairs
Henry Maynard of Vauxhall
Robert Lett of Westminster Horseferry
Robert Oliver of Deptford
Joseph Hill of Vauxhall

The above men were ordered to be at their respective stations, off the Old Swan Stairs, London Bridge, at half past three o'clock, to row from thence to the Swan at Chelsea, against tide – a most severe task for the young aspirants. They were at their places in due time. Cutters attended several. There were not many boats out on this occasion, for the afternoon being far from suspicious. A short time after four they were started; Carmarthy, who had the inside station, had the start, but instead of keeping his boat as much in shore as possible, he kept her head out. Hill, who was a close second, took advantage of this position, and coming on Carmarthy's quarter, turned him right athwart the tide. At this critical period, Maynard, who was bending his back at his work in good style, rowed bang upon Carmarthy's boat, and nearly swamped him. Indeed, if he had not jumped off his thwart, and leaned over on the starboard side of his boat, she must have sunk. This circumstance threw Carmarthy out of the match altogether; for had he afterwards obtained the lead, and arrived first at Chelsea, the fact of his rising from his thwart would have prevented him from claiming the Livery or any other prize. During the slight confusion that prevailed when fouling, Oliver went in advance; Maynard followed him along the Surrey shore, as second. Just below Westminster Bridge, Oliver who appeared to act under the guidance of those in his galley shot the *water for the Middlesex shore, which he gained in very good style. Maynard on the contrary, kept on the Surrey side, until he reached Honey and Archer's Roads, when he made over to his opponent on the opposite shore. He was, however, too much in the rear to cut him off, although we think that the course he took brought him nearer to the leading man. Colcomb was third up to the Horseferry, where Hill succeeded in exchanging places with him. The others were some distance astern. Between Waterloo and Vauxhall the men were overtaken by a heavy storm, which caused the water in a very few seconds to trickle down the legs of their trousers. It is rather a singular fact, that as the wagermen were rowing between the above Bridges in the preceding year, a heavy shower, similar in violence to the one of yesterday, came down upon them. Oliver succeeded with great difficulty in maintaining the lead, for Maynard closely pressed him, and ultimately won the Livery and Badge amid the cheers of the spectators assembled. Maynard, as second, became entitled to about £5, but the sum is regulated by the state of the funds- it sometimes falling short of the amount by a few shillings. Hill as third, and Colcomb as fourth, also received prizes in money. The two others rowed up to Vauxhall, and then resigned the contest. Among the watermen assembled yesterday we noticed several who had "years long past" won the Coat and Badge; and on the above occasion threw aside their usual apparel, and once again attired themselves in the Livery they had so nobly rowed for and won."*

It was not a particularly pleasant period in my life. But, I prayed that the weavers of destiny would grant me good fortune in two years time to help me achieve my ambitions of becoming the first Maynard to win the prestigious coat and badge.

Eventually, I received a telegram from John Crawford explaining that a resident from Cornwall had been arrested. But, due to a technicality, he had to be released – the technicality being that the suspect was already in jail in France when Murphy had been slain. Crawford assured me that other leads were being followed through, and I could expect some good news within days.

Sadly, no news came – good or bad.

Hill and Crawford obtained a warrant to keep the *Royal Fuetan* under supervision for a further two days, and no longer. The Admiralty Marshall's office was resolute that if no arrest was made within forty-eight hours, the ship would be released. Crawford continued questioning Trevaliant regarding who the woman was. But, it was clear that he knew nothing. Hill considered the possibility of quizzing both the mates and the engineer if the crew were in the clear. Hill's reasoning was sound – If the crew and the Captain were exonerated, the target had to be one of the officers. During the forty-eight hours available to Crawford, every junior officer played their parts well, swearing their innocence on their mother's lives. With their hands on their hearts, all three men pleaded not being guilty and totally blameless of any crime. The results of the investigation made Hill very frustrated. Like a dog tethered to a chain, he wanted to be set free to try his own mode of questioning. But, Crawford would hear none of it, knowing what it could lead to.

Crawford and Hill were alone in the cabin discussing what they knew and what they didn't know. The answer had to be connected with the Captain's wife; she had been there on the quayside, waiting to board the ship, and both Crawford and Hill had seen her climb the gangway into her husband's embrace.

"We have to question the Captain again, David," Crawford explained.

Hill had had enough of riddles, and begged Crawford to let him have ten minutes alone with Captain Froggy. He felt sure that he could make the man sing like a French canary. Crawford was tempted by the suggestion; he knew Hill was more than capable of getting results from his persuading fists. After all, Lord David Hill was the enforcer, a true legend as some said. However, Crawford remained resolute. There was to be no brutality on his watch, not until it was the last resort. They still had one more day of the warrant available.

Captain Martin entered the cabin, flanked by his two royal marine guards. When Crawford pointed to a chair, Martin responded by shrugging his shoulders, as if he couldn't be bothered if he sat or not. But, he decided to sit all the same. The Frenchman requested that he be asked questions in his native language, knowing that Crawford spoke fluent French. It appeared that he had little time for Hill, who he knew could not understand his answers. This was not going to be a good session.

'Bonjour, Capitaine,' Crawford commenced. Hill appeared to be content – so far, he understood what was being said.

'Pourquoi suis-je un prisonnier?' replied the captain. And, Lord Hill's smile vanished, he was lost.

'*Tu es mon invité,*' Crawford answered. With that, Hill left the cabin to get some air, or so he said.

'Comment va ta femme aujourd'hui?' enquired Crawford.

126

'Je n'ai pas de femme.'

The Frenchman's reply completely baffled Crawford.

"If you are not married, then who was the woman who greeted you so warmly upon your arrival?" he could not help but ask.

It was from this stage that both the questions and the answers of the interview continued in English.

The Frenchman assumed the woman to be either the wife or daughter of the agent.

"I can assure you Mr. Crawford, I have never married. I am away from home so much to enjoy the home comforts of a good woman."

Crawford nodded in agreement. He had been married for nearly forty years now, and he was a man who enjoyed his wife's company. The conversation forced Crawford to recall the passing of Lady Hill. The scars took years to heal. They had lived their lives as one, and, afterwards, he had been forced to limp along without support as an incapacitated individual.

Crawford was confident the French Captain was telling the truth, but if that was right, where should he direct his next line of questioning.

The French captain soon left the cabin with the royal marines by his side. However, Crawford suggested the captain be given liberty about the ship.

Crawford relaxed in his chair, formulating things inside his mind. The mystery woman, if indeed it was a woman, had to be the key to the matter. Secondly, Crawford weighed up inside his head whether it was a woman or a man. He finally came to the conclusion that the person who boarded the *Royal Fuetan* on docking had to be a man dressed in women's clothing. And, if that proved to be correct, had the ship's agent been an accomplice? Crawford had to consider that a seaman had died, and probably been substituted by the interloper. Eventually Crawford scribbled his thoughts down on paper in order of importance.

(1) Man dressed as woman embarks the Royal Fuetan.

(2) Seaman dies during voyage, and body is disposed of.

(3) Imposter takes the place of the seaman.

(4) Henry Trevaliant is in the clear.

(5) Unsure about Captain. Gut feeling tells me he is innocent. However, the captain should always be aware of matters below deck, especially if one of his crewmembers had died during the voyage to London. Perhaps, there was a simple explanation – but why had it been kept secret from the captain.

This gave rise to the question of whether there might have been an accomplice already concealed aboard the *Royal Fuetan* to offer assistance and protection to the newcomer.

Laws, a man of unrivalled credentials and a wiry old fox to boot, had always been persistent with his assumption that the French captain had been withholding vital information – a view shared by Lord Hill. Only Crawford, the spy master, stayed firm to his judgement that Captain Martin was innocent.

When Lord Hill returned to the cabin, Crawford asked him to check on the London agent; was he a bona fide, or should they be aware of any dubious business or marital misappropriations, whereby the agent might be the target of blackmail. He debated with himself, wondering whether he should add this on his list as yet unanswered question number six. But, he decided against it, considering that this question would soon be answered.

Before sunset, a message came back to the ship from the Horse Guards, confirming that the London agent was trustworthy and was held in high esteem among his fellows at the recently-established Baltic Exchange. Crawford hurriedly dismissed his intention of adding item six on his list, happy with the knowledge that the first three items on his list now would have to be thoroughly investigated again, with the remaining two placed on the back-burner. However, he still had to consider the possibility of an accomplice as a feasible suggestion.

Crawford had completely forgotten about a witness who could identify the murderer; he had told them that he spoke to the man. However, Crawford, the spy master, had overlooked this

129

fundamental clue, and Lord Hill, the legend and enforcer, had completely forgotten the statement.

Not receiving any solid information, John Crawford slid further down his chair. He reconsidered the mission that he recently sent Richard Sharpe to probe. But until the return of his good friend Crawford sat starring at the cabin ceiling totally alone in abject misery and despair.

CHAPTER 13

Telling white lies

Assuming that no one other than the agent had disembarked the *Royal Fuetan* during her short stay within Saint Katharine's Dock, Crawford's spies could only draw one conclusion – the offender was still onboard hiding within the ship. Or was he in plain sight, strolling confidently about the ship, daring anyone to approach him, especially Lord Hill and his marine guards?

Crawford was content with the knowledge that the ship had been searched, double-searched, and, in some cases, triple-searched. Every storage-locker had been checked for false panels, and every inch of the empty hold had been fully explored. So, he tried to relax. But, Crawford was not a happy man.

The marines poked their bayonets between the gaps of the timber frames and planks. But, no blood had shown itself on their steel blades so far. Lord Hill was confident that no living soul could find refuge within the beating heart of the *Royal Fuetan*. It made Hill wonder whether this sinister entity was living, or whether it was, perhaps, a phantom. Whatever the case, one thing was for sure – it had killed at least two people already. So, the lump of shit couldn't be a figment of his imagination or an illusion from the recesses of his dreams.

This left out just one scenario, which tormented Crawford's mind; the killer was in plain sight of everyone. And, that was disconcerting. Whoever it was, the killer was exceptionally confident. Hill and Crawford studied the faces of the crew members for any tell-tale signs that might have given the apparition away. The predator was pure evil; no doubt it enjoyed the constant scrutiny that was being served to it. If it did revel in the sheer delight of killing, it must surely be a psychopath, devoid of all emotions and having a complex soul, with a black heart pounding within its evil breast. If it was an animal, the veterinarian would have taken it down. And that was exactly what Crawford had in mind – to take the bastard down. Evil bred evil, and wickedness bred sin. This tormentor of souls was, without a shadow of doubt, someone who had slithered away from the filthy sewers of Satan. But, conquering this devil-form seemed near unattainable, unless the spinner ladies weaved their magic to cut through its thread of life.

Too much thinking made Crawford feel uncomfortable; he suddenly shuddered as if something or someone had just walked over his grave. Hill returned to the cabin, informing his friend that all appeared to be quiet. He was going to say "as quiet as the grave", but he decided that that would be in bad taste.

"David, I have decided to invite the three French officers to dine with us tonight."

Lord Hill was appalled at the suggestion of sharing food and drink with his adversaries; he voiced his objections at the thought of it. Crawford, however, requested that his friend should hear him out and be patient.

"I want to spread a chink of panic within their ranks, and I need you to stay onside and back me up on everything I say," suggested Crawford.

As no one on board was capable of cooking a decent meal, or restock the ship's empty wine locker, of good quality wine, port and brandy, Crawford sent for Solomon and Margaret Ribbens from the Three Daws to cook the evening meal for the six; three French officers, plus Lieutenant Gee, who commanded the Royal Marines, together with Crawford and Hill.

The purpose of the cosy dinner party was to tempt the fox to bolt from his lair and come out into the open. However, Crawford required Hill to back him up in order to make his plan work. Lord Hill was not enthusiastic about the merry-making. However, he always enjoyed the food that was served at the Three Daws. He, therefore, reluctantly agreed.

"Shall we agree that the meal should be served at nine, with pre-dinner drinks served at eight?"

Such timings allowed them three hours to get dressed into their formal dress uniforms. The invitations were sent-out, and Captain Martin, First Mate Bernard, and Second Mate Olivier all gladly accepted the invite, which pleased Crawford.

Lord David Hill explained to the Royal Marine Officer, Lieutenant Gee, to go along with everything that Crawford said or suggested, which he whole-heartedly agreed to. After all, he was being bribed by the smell of excellent home-cooking.

At eight o'clock, the small cabin began to fill up. Eventually, all six diners received their first drink, and polite conversation had commenced. Albeit, it was only one-sided with regards to Lord Hill since his expertise of the French language limited him. Crawford rose from his chair to give the first toast of the evening.

"Gentlemen, The King of England, and our gracious friends across the channel in France, long may they all live."

All the men drank without making too much of a fuss. Solomon Ribbens seemed happier now that he was serving six customers as opposed to his crowded tavern. As the drinks flowed, the smell of cooking began to filter its way into the cabin from the nearby galley. Captain Martin asked Lord Hill what was on the menu, to which Hill elegantly replied that wild mushroom soup, pigeon pie, spotted dick, and custard would be there to fill him, followed by cheese and biscuits. Hill reminded the captain that the dinner would end with coffee and brandy. Martin seemed suitably impressed and smacked his lips in relish, as if he was tasting the food already. He translated the menu for the benefit of his two French-speaking subordinate officers. Solomon Ribbens continued to serve his fine wines accompanied by large glasses of brandy. All the while, he kept calculating the bill in his mind for the end of the night – Solomon Ribbens was a crafty old sod, but he was a likeable old sod all the same.

"Shall we sit, gentlemen," Crawford suggested to his guests, "Dinner is about to be served."

Hill and Crawford witnessed the way in which the French ate. It was as if they hadn't eaten for weeks. They tucked into their food as if they were half-starved. They mopped up any surplus soup from their bowls with their freshly baked bread. Once the soup bowls were removed, new plates arrived, overflowing with the pigeon pie and fresh seasonal English vegetables. The conversations stalled for a while as good food became a priority. The only sounds that came from the French side of the table, besides the clinking of knife on fork, was the belches and burps matched in perfect harmony.

The spotted dick and cheese followed the pigeon pie in quick succession. Finally, the time came for brandy, port, and coffee – and, hopefully, lots of careless chatter. It was Crawford who began the conversation by asking how life was like in France, and how the weather was.

"An Englishman's favourite subject," laughed Captain Martin.

The English gave polite, if not forced laughs, whilst the French thought the subject to be hilarious. Crawford looked towards Solomon Ribbens and ordered more brandy for his guests. He remained sober throughout; careful not to drink too much alcohol. The Frenchmen, Lord Hill, and Lieutenant Albert Gee were all getting bouts of the giggles. Maybe it was time for Crawford to spread his little white-lies to liven up the proceedings.

"Gentlemen," Crawford started his smears, looking mainly towards the Captain Martin, "We have some good news for you. We have recently received news that will be most welcome to your ears. We have it on good authority that the counterfeiter known as Fauntleroy has been found in the City of London. It appears that his work is of the highest quality, better than anything anyone was attempting, and is only detectable by senior banking officials within the Bank of England. We shall leave your ship in peace in the morning, and you, my dear Captain, can return to France."

Hill intervened by slapping the table and breaking into a song. It was quite a torture since Hill could not sing. Crawford tried to plug his ears. It sounded as if a cat was being murdered.

The noise was horrendous.

CHAPTER 14

Lunch at Threadneedle Street

At the precise time at which Crawford was enjoying his dinner party aboard the *Royal Fuetan*, George Maynard was hard at work, rowing passengers backwards and forwards and across the river. However, when he was not engaged with a fare, he practised his skills that would be needed were he lucky enough to scull for Doggett's. Jimmy Kipper was always nearby, timing George's progress from the standing starts. Then, it was Kipper's turn to scull. Both the lads were careful not to collide with any structure or craft that obstructed their course. Henry, the brother of George Maynard who had participated two years earlier, had explained to both the lads that the importance of a good start was paramount.

Henry's second rule was to scull as if the devil himself was after you, and remembering to take instructions from your coaches. It was the coaches who would try to advise you in case you needed to alter course, thereby avoiding bridge abutments, or, worse, an outward-bound vessel.

In 1833, at least two-hundred and fifty first year freemen would apply to participate in the wager. The number would be reduced to just six, but the fortunate six competitors would not necessarily be the best six. They would, hopefully like me, be the luckiest six. The race would be held when the tidal current would be the strongest against them. It would take around four hours of muscle, sweat, determination, and a tremendous amount of luck to be successful and win the celebrated coat and badge of Thomas Doggett. It must be borne in mind that luck starts on the steps of Watermen's Hall in the drawing of lots. It, of course, ain't the fairest of ways to be one of the six. However, unless they came up with some other way to decide on the final six, it was up to Lady Luck to play her part. George and Kipper considered the odds, both recognising that skill alone would not be enough to row for Doggett's; it came down to pure luck to survive that first hurdle.

Meanwhile, back aboard a ship at anchor off Higham, Crawford enjoyed himself. He kept throwing one lie after another into the cauldron. However, the main point he needed to get across was to enlighten his guests that a master counterfeiter was at work, whose end-product was far superior to Henry Fauntleroy. Jealousy is a wondrous weapon to behold – it could lead you to annihilate your competitor, especially if they were better than you. And to top it all, Crawford told them that this forger was the best. Crawford boasted about and complimented the bogus printer for his printed money and bonds, insinuating that the bugger had made millions in the last week alone. Not a soul aboard the *Royal Fuetan* knew if Crawford's account was correct or not, with the vessel having been under arrest and anchored off shore for the past four days. Crawford told the French officers that the City bankers were panic stricken, not knowing which way to turn; it was the South Sea bubble all over again. In the midst of all this, Crawford had to be careful. He noticed the gloom descending on the faces of Hill and Gee. Had they played their parts too well? Or were they about to commit suicide with their savings about to be lost and become worthless?

138

Crawford decided to ease-off talking about dismal topics, in favour of partaking of a large glass of port and brandy. He stood, saluted, and toasted to all and sundry: "Gentlemen may we live long and prosper." Hill and Gee joined the toast. But, it was clear that the Frenchmen didn't know how to respond. They eventually stood, albeit on unsteady legs, and drank a bumper toast to a long life.

The following morning, Crawford, Hill, and Gee, together with his small company of Royal Marines, disembarked the *Royal Fuetan* to head for the Gravesend Terrace Pier. Once ashore, they ordered a watch on the ship to make sure that no person left the ship, except the pilot boat, and then to make sure it was only one person that was steering the small craft. All they could do now was to wait and watch.

The pilot cutter rowed out to the ship, boarded the channel pilot, and returned to Gravesend with one man on board. However, the man was considerably taller and heavier than the man who delivered the pilot. In the ensuing panic, men were running this way and that, without being particularly aware of what they were supposed to be doing. The fugitive took this opportunity to abscond into the shambolic mass of people, who had gathered by Terrace Pier. In the minutes that followed, numerous families of excursionists were embroiled within the throng of stampeding accumulation of humanity; no one knew who they were running to or away from. Self-control and calm had instantly faded before Crawford's eyes. The best-laid plans of mice and men had evaporated right in front of him, casting its dark shadow over his day. He should have been more vigilant. How could he possibly provide an explanation for a murderer vanishing right in front of him and a Company of Royal Marines?

Crawford had to think quickly. Hill had caught up with him in the foray, waiting attentively to act upon instructions. It was raw commotion that surrounded the two men; Crawford desperately needed time to think. Unfortunately, time was not on his side; the outrageous villain had got away clean.

"Bloody hell," Hill burst out, "There's going to be hell to play when we get back to Horse Guards."

"We are not going back to Horse Guards," Crawford declared, "We are going to the Bank of England at Threadneedle Street; as I am reasonably certain our adversary will be."

"How do we get back to the city with all this disarray about us?" Hill asked, looking around him to see that order had dissipated into chaos.

Crawford looked angrily at Hill, reminding him how they did it in Spain.

"We bloody stole the ponies!" came Hill's reply, "Better not do that now…Best to hire two mares of the four-legged variety. We don't want the Peelers chasing us."

It had struck three in the afternoon, as they entered the Bank of England, requesting to see the manager – only to be told that the manager was out with clients enjoying a late lunch. Lord Hill butted in to the conversation to ask where the manager normally dined to entertain his clients. The answer came back, although the clerk had failed to ask for either Crawford or Hill's identity, that the banker could probably be found at Mercer's. Lord Hill silenced the clerk, who was trying to explain the location, by bawling that he knew where the place was.

Crawford asked the clerk whether any other stranger had recently enquired where his manager might be, to which the clerk freely replied, "Yes…a French Sea Captain."

"Bugger it! You and Laws were right all along. Why didn't you correct me Hill?"

"You are the damn spy master," Lord David Hill smirked, "I am just the legend, the enforcer." However, under his breath Hill muttered, "Silly old bugger – we told him so."

The pair marched off together in the direction of Mercer's, a high class restaurant in Threadneedle Street. Lunch was almost over, and the waiters were clearing the tables of plates and empty glasses, removing the linen tablecloths, and getting ready for the night's reservations. Mercer's had always been popular with the banking classes; there was lots of money to be earned entertaining clients, if you were bold enough and had a wad full of bank notes in your pockets. However, the rewards were aplenty from future business and the lucrative bond markets.

You had to have plenty of money to walk through the door at Mercer's, and both Crawford and Hill looked bedraggled. How

141

they managed to get past the commissionaire was a miracle in itself. Perhaps, it was the threatening glare from the old army men.

Crawford noticed a small group of men, towards the rear of the establishment, who looked like bankers entertaining their clients – you could easily tell by the number of bottles and glasses remaining on the table.

"Let me talk, John," Hill asked, "After all, I am a titled individual of noble birth."

Lord David Hill requested a minute with the man at the head of the table, whom he thought to be one of the senior managers at the Bank of England. The man hesitated at first, ignoring Lord Hill. But, after a gentle shove from behind administered by his Lordship, he had gained the man's full attention; even though the man did not look over pleased with the way in which he had been interrupted. David Hill, the so-called legend and enforcer employed by John Crawford, got to work immediately, explaining to the banker that mischief was in the air.

"My name is Lord David Gordon Hill, David after a former King of Israel, Gordon after a famous general from north of the border, and Hill because that was his father's name. I have a noble title, and that entitles me to shove you and other inferior urchins around. And, what's more, the only people I answer to is this man by my side and the King of England."

This wasn't going well. Crawford had to intervene to remind Hill to be reasonable, if not polite. However, Lord Hill was in full sway and continued with his discourteous behaviour, since he intensely hated bankers. He referred to them as legal robbers, who had brought this great country to its knees one-hundred years ago. As far as Lord Hill was concerned, bankers were greedy and corrupt, and a blight on the landscape. Lord Hill noticed a half-full glass of brandy on the table before him, and he picked it up and devoured the contents in one gulp. David Hill was quite an optimist. In his vocabulary, nothing was half-empty, but always half-full.

Crawford decided to interrupt the conversation before trouble ensued; the disrupted conversation had already been noticed by nearby diners.

"Forgive my friend. My name is John Crawford. I am in charge of counter-espionage at Horse Guards, and Lord David Hill has already introduced himself. We are here on a matter of high urgency that concerns the King, the country, and counterfeit money," declared Crawford.

The bank manager remained uninterested, until Hill shoved him again to remind him that he was being spoken to by highly-ranked intelligence officers, answerable only to the Crown. In other words, he was simply asking the banker, "Pay full attention when either of us converses with you."

Hill politely requested everyone, with the exception of the fear-stricken banker to leave the table. Crawford later, however, gave another version to the court while being under oath – Hill had ordered the men to sod off! Hill couldn't care less, nor did the court of enquiry.

"Now we are completely alone," Crawford continued, "Has anyone else tried to make contact with you today related to counterfeit money?"

They never discovered the bank manager's name, as Hill had decided that his name was irrelevant, and I suppose it was. Crawford and Hill waited for the answer, but as none was forthcoming, a further prod into the banker's ribs did the trick. The banker started to talk more freely with his answers coming in a lot quicker.

"Someone requested an urgent meeting for this afternoon, explaining that he wished to deposit large sums of money into the bank. He insisted to know about our security arrangements; in fact, I should be meeting him in half an hour."

Crawford demanded to know the name of the person whom he would be meeting. However, the banker couldn't remember the name, except for the fact that it sounded Cornish. The banker spluttered out the name "Trevalier" or something very similar; by now, the banker was fearful for his life. He found himself outside his comfort zone, alienated by men who spoke with their fists, and prodded with their elbows – it was an unpleasant experience, one that he had never encountered before and didn't want to experience again.

Crawford and Hill, satisfied that as no other information was pertinent, suggested that the banker remain inside Mercer's restaurant to enjoy another glass of brandy, or two! "Just write a note explaining to your cashier that this afternoon's interview with our Cornish friend will be conducted by Messrs Crawford and Hill."

And so it was, the clock, hanging on the wall in the banker's office ticked away to its heart's content. Crawford, found it to be irritating due to the noise it was making. He settled back into the banker's chair, trying to relax.

The clock showed ten minutes to four, and he hoped that the case would be resolved in a matter of just ten minutes. The office was spacious and decorated to a high standard with plush carpets, drapes, and tasteful pictures hanging on the walls. Lord Hill had placed himself by the far wall, behind the opening door that opened inwards, just in case Crawford needed assistance. Crawford checked the clock again – three minutes to four. He could feel his heart pounding inside his chest. The hair on the back of his neck stood on their end. But, what bothered him the most was that he was sweating profusely. He wondered whether it was a sign of nerves or heightened adrenaline – whatever the cause, the answer would be revealed soon.

Even though Crawford was expecting a knock on the door, he instinctually jumped out of his skin to such an extent that he found the word 'enter' hard to pronounce when he had to say it. He finally managed to say the word out, but it sounded as if he was gargling with whisky. The door opened to reveal a surprised Henry Thomas Trevaliant, the supposed freed prisoner from Paris. The look of surprise quickly evaporated from his face to reveal a sinister grin, which quickly turned into a snarl.

145

Trevaliant didn't utter a word as he walked at a snail's pace into Crawford's temporary office. The Cornishman, or whoever he was, moved a chair from the opposite side of the desk to where Crawford was sitting. He wanted to make himself comfortable and relaxed, ready to receive any taunts and hurl any abuse back. Trevaliant looked very self-assured and confident. But, had he noticed that Hill was quietly sitting back against the wall, no more than twelve feet behind him.

Trevaliant began to boast how easy it had been to fool Crawford's dim-witted team, how effortless it would have been to slit their throats had he the desire to do so, and how easily he escaped from the chaos of Gravesend. "I could go on, Mister Crawford," Trevaliant said, "But, I don't want to embarrass you too much."

Crawford wondered if he could tempt the Cornishman to admit to his crimes, asking whether John Maynard and Patrick Murphy were murdered by his obnoxious hands. Trevaliant leant back in his chair and freely confessed to his wickedness. He even confessed to killing Captain Martin before taking his place in the tender boat that brought him ashore to Terrace Pier, "It is very easy to extinguish life, Mister Crawford. The poor old waterman who rowed me ashore found it most difficult to die. I had to poke him with my blade five times before he went to his maker. And, I kicked him overboard to help him on his way to visit Neptune."

Trevaliant produced a four-inch steel blade from his waistcoat pocket and began using it as a toothpick. I think his intention was to stir up Crawford's emotions; the evil piece of excrement actually wanted Crawford to challenge him. As Trevaliant continued with his boasting, he hadn't heard Hill slowly

146

creeping towards him from the rear, until a knock on the door made him fully alert. By then, it was too late. Hill punched the side of his impudent face, which felled him like a sack of potatoes.

Crawford knew that the legend packed a punch. But, after witnessing Hill's sledge-hammer of a blow, he decided not to agitate him in the future.

Hill asked Crawford whether he suspected Trevaliant prior to him entering the banker's office, to which Crawford replied that a true-bred Cornishman would know that Brixham was in Devon - not Cornwall, and that little error was what had first intrigued him. In addition, it was only Trevaliant who informed us about a fellow seaman dying from a fever, and Crawford admitted that he considered it strange that Captain Martin failed to mention this fact.

As Trevaliant lay unconscious on the office carpet, Crawford and Hill disarmed the man. Besides the knife that he had flashed at Crawford during their short conversation, Trevaliant carried two other knives – one with a serrated edge. In addition to those, he had on himself a pistol and a short metal club. Trevaliant was truly an evil bastard, one of the worst. The man was past redemption. He had no just cause to fight for, outside of the fact that he enjoyed seeing his victims suffer. I think he enjoyed stirring up trouble, be it revolution or something else.

Soon after, Robert Peel entered the room to survey the scene for himself. He scrutinised the man spread-eagled on the floor before him; all he could see was a slaughterer of the innocent, a slayer of the blameless. Peel turned away from Trevaliant, he had seen enough. He glanced at John Crawford and Lord David Hill and offered a cheeky smile and said two words – "Well done" He twisted round to speak to his sergeant, "Read this trash his rights."

Peel warmly shook hands with Crawford and Hill before leaving.

The trial of Henry Thomas Trevaliant was fixed for Monday, the fourteenth of November 1831. However, the prisoner refused to enter a plea. He even refused his legal right for counsel. In fact, he refused everything - even refusing to acknowledge his name or abode. The trial continued with the judge stating, "Henry Thomas Trevaliant, or whatever name you wish to be recognised as, of no fixed abode, on the following dates – you wilfully murdered – the full names were given to the court reporter. How do you plead?"

Silence............

There was no reply. Only an evil grin spread across the Cornishman's face. They failed to ascertain whether he was Cornish or not. He desperately tried to appear arrogant and conceited. But, I wondered if his stoic facade would remain when the gallows of Newgate came in focus.

The trial ended, and the judgement was passed – hang by the neck until dead. However, Trevaliant still appeared defiant. He was taken down to the cells, and three days later, Trevaliant became acquainted with the noose on a bright sunny morning. Crawford desperately tried to uncover the answers to his questions that haunted him for the past few months. But, the Cornishman steadfastly remained voiceless.

He remained defiant even when the noose was gathered tightly about his neck, not even shouting out a single word when the lever opened the trapdoor.

Whatever his motives were, no one would ever really know. Whether he tried copying Fauntleroy remained a mystery. But, I will tell you one thing – when his neck was eventually stretched, he pissed and shit his trousers. I was glad it was not me who had to clean up the mess. On occasions, the prison wardens assisted the condemned man to pass to his God quicker by pulling down hard on his legs. However, that was not the case for Trevaliant – no one rushed forward to help Trevaliant to shake hands with the devil.

CHAPTER 15

The glorious first

Our whole family followed the newspaper reports of the trial with great interest. Even though the reporters couldn't write that much since the accused had failed to cooperate with the authorities – he did not provide his name or offer a plea. It was then that, for the first time, I explained to my family about my part in the apprehension of the ghoul. At first, they were shocked. But, eventually they came to accept my reasoning. Trevaliant's trial didn't last too long before his sentence was passed – death by hanging. Crawford and Lord Hill reported back to me after witnessing the hanging. I am thankful to them for leaving out all the gory bits. Whoever the evil villain was, he went slowly to his death a nameless individual.

One year later, on the eighth day of November in 1832, I attended Waterman's Hall, hopefully for my final examination; I was going up for my freedom. Uncle George, together with my parents, joined us to give moral support, or, perhaps, sympathy should I fail in my freedom. The court was opened by the Master of the Company, who along with five or six other court examiners asked the usual questions regarding the names of the plying places of the watermen, the tide sets at the various bridges, plus numerous other questions of which I felt confident that I had answered correctly. The clerk of the court requested me to retire from the parlour room for a short time. On my return, my prayers were answered – I had completed my seven-year apprenticeship, and now I was a freeman, a man to be looked up to. Mother and father were so very happy for me, as was my master and uncle, George Wyld.

In June of 1833, George Maynard and James Kippen, two first year freemen, attended a gathering at the Watermen's Hall, the purpose of which was to draw lots to ascertain the names of the six first-year freemen who would row for Doggett's coat and badge on the first of August 1833. Only those first-year freemen who had gained their freedom since the second day of August 1832 were allowed to put forward their names. The spinners of destiny must have looked down kindly on me that day, and my prayers were granted again. My name was successfully drawn as a participating lot from a list of nearly two-hundred-and-fifty. The other names drawn were John Butcher from Hungerford, George Harding from Horselydown, John Pullinger from Fountain Stairs, Charles Cripps from Richmond and William Prior from Battersea. Sadly there was no winning lot for James Kippen. Everyone was looking for the name of Robert Newell from Saint Olave's, Southwark. Had he had been offered the same degree of luck as me; he would have most certainly been the favourite to win the wager. Fortunately for me, his name failed to appear on the list of six finalists.

The glorious first of August fell on a Thursday in 1833, with the vast majority of the country celebrating the commemoration of the happy accession of the present Family of His Majesty to the throne of Great Britain – it seemed like a public holiday. Thomas Doggett, the famous comedian, who had died in 1721 at Eltham, in the county of Kent, left money in his will for the continuation of the race that bore his name. The watermen and lightermen always shouted out his name on the glorious first, in honour and recognition of the man.

In addition to the beautiful orange coat and silver arm badge, other monetary prizes had been established, thanks to the late Sir William Jolliffe.

Henry and Elizabeth Maynard, together with their extended families, made their way to Swan Pier, by London Bridge, to board one of the cutters so that they could follow the race. Henry Maynard noticed numerous past winners of the race, which Doggett had initiated in 1715, sporting their livery with pride. However, the present day's contest had caused immense congestion along the line of the river through which the contestants had to pass. Charles Cripps from Richmond failed to arrive at the start and was declared void.

Every vantage point was chock-a-block, including the newly-built London Bridge and the old bridge at Westminster. The noise was deafening at six o'clock, when the six competitors drew alongside their stake boats opposite the Old Swan, abreast of Fishmongers' Hall, for words of encouragement together with their final instructions before the umpire raised his pistol to signify the start of the contest.

At twenty past six, when the tide began ebbing, the pistol banged out aloud, signalling the race to commence.

George Maynard, who had the in-shore station, went in advance, closely followed by Harding and Pullinger. In shooting over at Southwark Bridge, Maynard continued to have an advantage over the others, with Harding close upon his quarter; but when passing under the shore arch, the latter fouled the pier. In an attempt to clear himself, Harding broke his oar. It was Pullinger then, who became second, and he severely contested the remainder of the distance with Maynard. They shot the Lambeth shore closely in the wake of each other. But, Maynard gallantly maintained his advantage, in spite of being desperately pressed by Pullinger. The scullers arrived opposite the Swan, at Chelsea, only about half a minute ahead of the below-bridge man, who ranked first favourite among the watermen in his part of the river at 3 to 2.

George Maynard received the coat and badge, valued at about ten shillings. John Pullinger, finishing second, received a cash prize. John Butcher came home third, with George Harding fourth, and William Prior fifth.

George rowed over towards Chelsea Pier to receive the adulations of his supporters. To his surprise, George noted the presence of John Crawford, Lord David Hill, Michael Laws, Joseph and Thomas Masters, Christian Bullas as well as Charlie Peek; they were all celebrating his victory alongside George Maynard's supporters. The merry-making continued well into the evening at the George Inn at Southwark.

This must have been the first time that I had legally been allowed to drink. To be honest with you, I felt quite uncomfortable. The entire tavern kept spinning before me, and my eyes ached like hell. I even began hallucinating. I was positive I identified Uncle John and Patrick Murphy clapping their hands in time with the celebrations. Following these ramblings, I thought I recognised Sir Richard sitting inside the tavern with an old soldier beggar sitting beside him. I rubbed my eyes as the apparition slowly came into focus; it looked like he was walking towards me with his arms open, as if to hug me, whilst the beggar remained in his seat.

Crawford and Hill came to my rescue by hugging Sir Richard – all three men were laughing together. Crawford looked at Sir Richard and said, "Glad you could make it Richard." So, I was not dreaming! Everything was unfolding before my weary eyes. Sir Richard turned to me saying, "Wouldn't have missed this for the world. Well done, George." John Crawford asked Richard who his ragged friend was.

"Oh I nearly forgot, this is Mister Henry Thomas Trevaliant, late of La Force Prison on the outskirts of Paris," replied Richard.

Sir Richard explained that the genuine Trevaliant had been secretly transferred from one jail to another on the instructions of a corrupt warden. Richard rightly assumed that this had been done to cover Trevaliant's tracks before he voyaged to England in order to start his reign of terror in the hope of stoking up revolutionary thoughts.

I was confused by all this – if this man is the real Henry Thomas Trevaliant, then who did we send to the gallows? Sir Richard shrugged his shoulders, as if he couldn't care less. Crawford and Hill came to join us. Nobody cared who the revolutionary was, and it appeared no one could give a damn - they were all grateful that he had been disposed off, cut out like a cancer.

All Sharpe said was, "if you have erected a headstone with a name upon it, I suggest you buy a replacement."

Had the spinners of destiny played any part in the arrest of the unknown man or led to his ultimate extinction due to his revolutionary beliefs? We will never know. Perhaps, if we tossed a coin, we would have got the same result. However, I preferred to believe in fate – good and bad.

HISTORICAL

NOTES

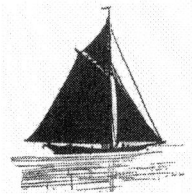

The weather conditions in 1825, as described within the first paragraph of the book, are historically accurate. The weather was extremely prone to change back then, with heavy storms at the beginning of the year, followed by a hot summer, gales in August, and snow in October.

George Wyld became the master to George Maynard on the thirteenth day of October, and Wyld was uncle to George through his marriage to Martha Maynard. George's father did not apprentice his son. It was possibly because his eldest son had drowned whilst passing under Westminster Bridge.

John Maynard was a customhouse waterman, and he did die when his boat collided with a barge, whilst both were passing under the London Bridge.

The binding years for George Maynard's father and grandfather are accurate. The Maynard family is intricately linked to the Thames over many generations.

When an apprentice was bound, it was his duty to prove that he was over fourteen, but not more than twenty years of age. Proofs of birth or baptism were recorded in the affidavit books.

In clinker-built boats, the edges of the hull planks overlap. Shorter planks can be joined end to end in order to make a longer strake or hull plank. By contrast, carvel-constructed vessels have planks butted smoothly – seam on seam.

Salmon, while it has become cheaper with the introduction of fish farms, remains a luxury item. During the years that this book portrays, salmon was abundant in the rivers of England, and it was a very cheap food. It is a fact that in major towns and cities, including London, there were laws preventing apprentices from being fed salmon more than three times a week!

Like George Maynard, James Kippen did exist. He was bound to his father on the same day. Both lads hailed from Lambeth, and it is reasonable to suggest that they might have been friends. However, the idea of the pair rowing downstream to Gravesend and back is purely fiction.

River folk repeatedly use nicknames, and Kipper, a name that dates back to at least 1599, seems to be most appropriate for young James Kippen. However, the term Mayday only came into existence in 1923, when a radio officer at Croydon Airfield was asked to come up with an appropriate word indicating the sender was in distress. The word derives its meaning from the French expression – m'aider, which means "help me". I trust the reader to excuse me for bringing the term "mayday" forward by one-hundred years.

Both Solomon and Margaret Ribbens were real characters, with Solomon holding the license for the Three Daws in 1826.

Late in the fifteenth century, around the year 1488, a group of unemployed ship carpenters constructed a row of cottages overlooking the river at Gravesend. Five hundred years later, the structure still stands under the sign of "The Three Daws". The carpenters used whatever timber they could lay their hands on, and every door, window, room, and cupboard was unique in size and shape. As the cottages were joined up, the random nature of the many staircases became more apparent, adding character to the structure.

In 1565, seven years after Queen Elizabeth I came to the throne, the inn first gained its license, which it has held ever since.

Merchant ships and men-o-war used to await the change of the tide at Gravesend; they could then take advantage of the current to carry them upstream. Experienced pilots would board the ships to guide them through the mud flats and shallows. Eventually, a pilot's house was built next to the tavern – a natural place to exchange tales of seamanship over a tankard of ale.

During the Stewart era, imported spirits were heavily taxed, and smuggling was highly profitable. The Three Daws was not averse to increasing its profits from these activities even though the Customs House was eventually built across the road. It is said to this day that if the walls of the cellars' were pulled down, tunnels would be found radiating out from the pub.

On the twenty-first day of January 1793, King Louis XVI was executed in Paris. Within a fortnight, Britain was at war with revolutionary France. King George III ordered press gangs to be sent out to bring experienced seamen into the Navy and to recover deserters.

Freemen and apprentices from the Watermen's Company, which being a guild without livery, were not protected from the clutches of the press gang. Only livery company members enjoyed that privilege. The only protection for the watermen and lightermen was if they were employed by the church or nobility, and in latter times when insurance companies dealing with riverside properties were established.

The Three Daws was regularly visited by the press gangs, but sailors loved the warren of staircases that increased their chance of escape. In 1798, a local order was passed that press gangs should only raid the tavern when two teams of the King's men were available.

By the start of the eighteenth century, a complex network of buildings had sprung up around the original Gravesend Blockhouse. It had a pier, a dock, and two wharves alongside, with a large house designed by the King's brother, James the Duke of York. After his return to England, King Charles, ordered the garrison be manned by a sergeant, twenty soldiers, and a gunner on loan from Tilbury Fort, in addition to the two lines of around twenty guns stretching on either side along the river. The blockhouse itself was no longer used to mount guns; but acted instead as the magazine for a wider fortification, being able to store 2,500 barrels of gunpowder.

Under the terms of the Peace of Utrecht in 1713, the artillery pieces had been reduced to ten. A survey conducted fifty years later reported that the Gravesend blockhouse remained in good condition and was subsequently equipped with ten nine pounder guns.

All that remains of the Gravesend blockhouse today

Amid rising concerns over the threat of a French invasion, Sir Thomas Page surveyed the blockhouse in 1778 and concluded that, in view of them being closely packed together, they could not easily fire downstream. Sir Thomas proposed that a larger fort be built further downstream to rectify this problem. The New Tavern Fort was constructed shortly afterwards, and the eastern Gravesend Blockhouse gun platform was redesigned and extended as part of the work. Two volunteer militia companies, established in 1794 and 1797, supported the blockhouse. In 1805, the blockhouse was equipped with nineteen thirty-two pounder guns. Concerns continued to be raised, because the guns could not fire downstream. By the early nineteenth century, the military decided to focus any future investment within the New Tavern and Tilbury Forts.

The blockhouse fell out of use as a magazine in 1834, and it was briefly used as a military store. The adjacent gun platforms were sold off during the following year, with the building subsequently demolished nine years later.

The weather in 1826 was as it has been described within these pages. The Thames did freeze as far downstream as Deptford, and partially at Greenwich. However, a prolonged hot summer commenced at the end of May, remaining for many months.

William Martin and his bumboat, the *Henrietta* named after his wife, all existed. The Martin family originated from the Northfleet and Gravesend areas. Just like the Maynard family, they could trace their roots through numerous generations of watermen. I know this owing to the fact that William Martin is my wife's third great-grandfather. The meaning of the word "bumboat" takes its import from a small wooden boat used to ferry supplies to ships anchored or buoyed offshore. Originally, it referred to a scavenger's boat; being derived from the Dutch word for a canoe, "boomschuit"; "boom" meaning tree, and boat.

The expression "piss-off" may only have come into being during the late 1940's. However, the expression, or certainly one with a similar meaning must have existed during the 1820's.

In Norse mythology, three female beings ruled the destiny of Gods and men. They roughly correspond to the controllers of the destiny of humans, such as the "Fates" in European mythology. The three spinners were depicted as weavers of a tapestry having their threads, or the breaking of threads, dictating the destinies of men.

The banknote (often known as a bill, paper money, or simply a note) is a type of negotiable promissory note, made by a bank, payable to the bearer on demand. Banknotes, originally issued by commercial banks, were legally required to be exchanged for legal tender, usually gold or silver coin, when presented to the chief cashier of the originating bank. When first introduced in England during the latter part of the eighteenth century, paper money resulted in a dramatic rise in forgery and counterfeiting.

The account of the real Henry Fauntleroy's trial and execution is accurate. Most crimes involve a conspiracy. In this case, a wholly unfounded rumour was widely credited to the effect that Fauntleroy had escaped strangulation by inserting a silver tube in his throat, and he escaped to have a life of comfort abroad. I have added my own angle to this conspiracy by adding the rumour concerning the Neckinger.

162

The crime of forgery ceased to become a capital offence in the mid 1830's. Lancelot Cooper was compared to Fauntleroy by *The Times* newspaper in 1827. Cooper was also condemned to death, but he, subsequently, had his sentence commuted to transportation, probably due to the influence of John FitzGibbon, the second Earl of Clare. The case of the supposed Henry Thomas Trevaliant in 1832 is pure fiction.

The family names and nicknames quoted in Bill Martin's list of suspects are all fictitious. My sincere apologies if I have caused any offence to any of the surnames mentioned.

A Jacob's ladder is a portable ladder made of rope, and it is used primarily as an aid in boarding ships. The name alludes to the Biblical Jacob, who is reputed to have dreamt that he climbed a ladder to heaven.

A manifest or customs manifest or "cargo document" is a document listing the cargo, passengers, and crew of a ship, for the use of customs and other officials.

During the great plague of London in 1665, the city remained sealed off, thereby avoiding contamination, and, hence, starvation became prevalent. The only people willing to trade with London were the Dutch sailors. The inhabitants of the city left money on the end of jetties, and the Dutch sailors braving the plague replaced the money with food. It is because of this that tens or even hundreds of thousands of lives were saved from starvation.

Interestingly, the Dutch sailors plied themselves with liquor before the perilous drop, as they believed that this would protect them from the plague as well as serving to steady their nerves a little! Thus, the expression *Dutch courage* was born.

Interestingly, the Dutch still have the freedom of the River Thames, which was granted as a reward for their courage and kindness during the great plague by the Mayor of London.

The expression "chalky" has been a long-established nickname for men born in the Swanscombe and Gravesend areas of Kent. The name originates from the chalky river banks found in abundance in the area.

The Neckinger is one of London's lost rivers. It earned its name from a macabre installation near its mouth at St Saviour's Dock, where a gibbet was erected for the execution of convicted pirates. The location became known as the Devil's Neckerchief, and the nickname soon echoed the river flowing out into the Thames. The monks of Bermondsey Abbey reclaimed and drained the land around the outflow of the Neckinger while embanking and enlarging the main outflow to form St Saviour's Dock.

The definition of "moonlighting" is to take on a second job that is separate from your main source of income.

Prior to the building of a permanent custom house at Gravesend, the tidewaiters made use of various riverside taverns in order to carry out their vital work, among the foremost of which was the Fountain Hotel.

The Fountain Hotel, Gravesend

Notice the windows of the upper storey offered
excellent panoramic views of the River Thames.

The purpose-built customhouse at Gravesend
erected on the site of the Fountain Tavern.

The Company of Watermen and Lightermen were somewhat of a closed shop, where membership was gained usually by form of servitude. The people worked hard to preserve restrictive practices for their members. This meant that other occupations were dependant on time served men. The river was the main trade route of the country, and vessels moving up the Thames from Gravesend were required to take the services of a freeman. Furthermore, a barge coming up and going through the bridges was compelled, if it needed a third hand, to take a waterman or lighterman.

Charles Dickens Junior said in 1887 "...vested interests are indeed wonderful institutions, and singularly tenacious of life!"

The term "King's evidence" vis to give information (such as the names of other criminals) to a court in order to reduce one's own punishment when one has been charged with a crime.

The rate books for the Jamaica Tavern show the licensee to be Thomas Cross during the time in which this novel has been set.

I am most grateful to Mr. Bernard Cornwell for allowing me to take liberties with the character he created – Richard Sharpe. Mr. Cornwell added, "It's most unlikely that Sharpe would be ennobled with a knighthood."

The French Revolution started in 1789 mainly due to the causes outlined in this novel. The only redeeming factor that was in England's favour was a stable government. In 1793, King Louis XVI and Marie Antoinette met with their premature deaths at the blade of the guillotine. In 1799, the remnants of the revolution were extinguished probably due to the success of General Bonaparte on the battlefields of Europe.

Thomas Paine was an English-born American political activist, philosopher, political theorist, and revolutionary. Born in Thetford in the English county of Norfolk, Paine migrated to the British American colonies in 1774 with the help of Benjamin Franklin, arriving just in time to participate in the American Revolution. Paine lived in France for most of the 1790's, becoming deeply involved in the French Revolution. The British government of William Pitt the Younger, worried by the possibility that the French Revolution might spread to England, had begun suppressing works that espoused radical philosophies.

Paine's work, which advocated the right of the people to overthrow their government, was duly targeted with a writ for his arrest issued in early 1792. Paine fled to France in September, where, rather immediately and despite not being able to speak French, he was elected to the French National Convention. The Girondists regarded him as an ally. Consequently, the Montagnards, especially Maximilien Robespierre, regarded him as an enemy.

Thomas Paine died at the age of seventy-two in Greenwich Village, New York City.

During the early nineteenth century, the period portrayed within this novel, London was the capital of the largest empire that the world had ever known, and it was infamously filthy. It had choking, sooty fogs. The River Thames was thick with human sewage; with the streets covered with mud and horse dung. The begging population of London has been estimated in the tens of thousands, especially after the Irish migration to England following the first potato blight in 1846. Even though begging was considered a crime, many beggars from the slums of London got round this predicament by entertaining their benefactors by playing musical instruments or selling mundane items such as clothes pegs. I have taken the liberty of bringing forward the potato famine by fifteen years.

On 23 March 1829, the Duke of Wellington and the Earl of Winchelsea fought a duel at Battersea Fields in South London. At this time, the Duke of Wellington was the Prime Minster of Great Britain and Ireland, and his Tory Government had passed the Catholic Relief Bill. This act represented the legislative move towards Catholic emancipation, and a section of the legislation would allow Catholics to take a seat in parliament. Wellington (who had been born in Dublin) had not initially been a supporter of Catholic Emancipation, but the fear of rebellion led him to change his views on the subject. Clearly, he was a pragmatist.

Conversely, The Earl of Winchelsea, was a staunch Protestant, and he accused *'The Iron Duke'* of an insidious design for the infringement of our liberties and the introduction of Popery into every department of the State. Insulted by this slur on his integrity, Prime Minster Wellington challenged Winchelsea to a duel, which Winchelsea accepted.

The newspaper report printed within this novel is most accurate, and it appeared in virtually every newspaper of the day.

Delope is a French word meaning, "throwing away". It refers to the practice of throwing away one's first fire in a pistol duel in an attempt to abort the conflict. According to most traditions, the *deloper* must first allow his opponent the opportunity to fire after the command ("present") is issued by the second, without hinting at his intentions.

Mrs. Maynard's reply to her son is with reference to the American Alexander Hamilton, a 19th-century American politician, who is thought to have attempted to *delope* during his infamous duel on 11th July 1804 with Aaron Burr, the then sitting Vice President of the United States. Rather than firing into the ground (as was customary for *deloping*), Hamilton fired into the air over Burr's head. Burr, perhaps misunderstanding his opponent's intent, fired directly at Hamilton, mortally wounding him. However, Burr's animosity towards Hamilton was such that it is not out of the question that Burr understood what Hamilton was doing and intentionally shot to kill.

In 1829, Sir Robert Peel, the then Home Secretary, established a new force to police London and the Home Counties. The first thousand of Peel's police were dressed in blue tail-coats and top hats, and they began to patrol the streets of London on 29th September 1829. The uniform was carefully selected to make the *'Peelers'* look more like ordinary citizens, rather than a red-coated soldier with a helmet.

The *'Peelers'* were issued with a wooden truncheon carried in a long pocket in the tail of their coat, a pair of handcuffs, and a wooden rattle to raise the alarm. By the end of the nineteenth century, the rattle had been replaced by a whistle.

Napoleon's downfall didn't take place at Waterloo at all! The battle was actually fought on the ground between the village of Mont St. Jean (the name by which the French know the engagement) in the north, and the inn called La Belle Alliance (the name by which it was known to the Prussians and is still known in Germany) in the south. But, on the day after the battle, when Wellington wrote his report, he did so at an inn in the village of Waterloo. Hence, it has been known as the Battle of Waterloo.

Today, it is hard to believe that Britain did not have a professional police force in the 18th century. Today, all policemen are commonly referred to as 'Bobbies' in Britain! Originally, they were known as 'Peelers' in reference to Sir Robert Peel.

Saint Katharine's Dock at night

'*To smell a rat*' is to recognize that something is not as it appears to be or that something dishonest is happening. This phrase has been in regular use within the English language since the early eighteenth century.

The first telegram service was opened in Great Britain in the year 1845. I have taken the liberty of bringing it forward to 1830/31.

The weather, as reported at the beginning of chapter 12, is completely accurate. There was a spectacular Christmas, followed by dense fog, and a mini ice age. There seems to be very little in the way of a summer, with constant rain and tremendous thunderstorms being reported during the first week in August. Frost fairs were held on the Thames during the months of January and February. It was fun for some, but misery for those who earned their living on the water. Due to the Thames being frozen, no ships or barges entered the Pool of London.

Fuddling tents were tents that were hastily constructed structures built from timber and sailcloth to offer protection from the low temperatures that Londoners experienced during the frost fairs.

The Baltic Exchange can trace its history back to 1744, when merchants and ship-owners traded in coffee exchanges at Threadneedle Street. It was formally set up in 1823 to combat wild gambling in the commodity markets, with formal rules being laid down.

'Walking over a grave' is an eighteenth century saying that derives from a much earlier folk legend. It refers to a sudden cold sensation caused by someone walking over the place that one's grave was eventually going to be. This belief is in line with the workings of people's minds in England during the middle ages, when the distinction between life and death was less clear than we see it now.

Henry Thomas Trevaliant is a fictional name, dreamt up by me. There was no trial and, therefore, no hanging.

The three spinners of destiny and fate

Printed in Great Britain
by Amazon